The Rebel Christian Publishing

ISBN: 9781957290386 (eBook)
Print: 9781957290393

This is a work of fiction. Any references to historical events, real
people, or real places are used fictitiously. Names, characters, and
places are products of the author's imagination. Inclusion of or
reference to any Christian elements or themes are used in a fictitious
manner and are not meant to be perceived or interpreted as an act of
disrespect against such a wonderful and beautiful belief system.

Cover image provided by Envato Elements, edited/altered by Valicity
Elaine

The Rebel Christian Publishing LLC
350 Northern Blvd STE 324 - 1390
Albany, NY 12204-1000

Visit us: http://www.therebelchristian.com/
Email us: rebel@therebelchristian.com

Contents

Series Order

MAGOG
The Rise of Desolation
The One Who is Man and Beast
The Broken Seals
The Darkest Hour

Other Books by A Bean
The End of the World (Christian End Times series)
Singlehood (Christian Romance)
The Woof Pack (Christian Romantic Suspense trilogy)
The Living Water (Christian Contemporary Fiction)
The Scribe (Christian Historical Fantasy)

MAGOG

Book I in the Ordained Catastrophe Saga

By A. Bean

A Rebel Christian Publishing Book

AUTHOR'S NOTE

Zombies are not real. The Bible is very real, but zombies are not. In no way is my work an outline of the Book of Revelation. It is a work of fiction that depicts adventure, love, and fear in the fashion of entertainment. Please read at your own risk. If the thought of zombies during the Biblical apocalypse is too farfetched, please feel free to read my other end times series, The End of the World, which features no zombies whatsoever.

I also want to mention that this series is not to incriminate any man, person, being, country, or religion. It is a work of fiction, ideas I pulled together with the Holy Spirit's influence to produce a story for readers. Surely there are things to gain from this, but this depiction is just another go at end times fiction. I am not, in any way, saying that the events in the Book of Revelation will unfold the way I describe, or happen according to the timeline I created for this book. Please refer to the Bible for accuracy, not my work.

As a Christian author, it is my duty to glorify God first, and present fiction in a respectful way second. Please remember that as you go forward.

1

You Will Devise an Evil Scheme

Keoni

"Kiki... Kiki..."

"Hmm?" I groaned as I rolled over.

"You're phone's ringing, baby."

I took a deep breath and let out another grunt as I reached for my phone. It was vibrating on the nightstand, lights flickering. Squinting, I stared at the screen.

Ollie.

The sight of his name immediately woke me up. I stiffened right there in bed.

"I-I have to take this," I said as I threw the covers back.

"Alright." Jensen lazily rolled over. Sleep was far more important to him than figuring out who was calling the love of his life at this hour. Sometimes Jensen was a little too trusting.

1

I crossed the floor into the bathroom, by the time I gently closed the door behind me, the phone had stopped ringing. But there were four missed calls from Ollie, so I knew he'd call again. We'd agreed not to contact each other unless it was urgent.

I was with Jensen now. The distance between Ollie and me had been good for us. But now he'd broken our agreement and had called me. Four times. Before sunrise.

I leaned against the counter, scrolling my phone in the early morning hours. Ollie hadn't sent any texts, which meant it was serious. Too serious for anything more than a few phone calls on the record. It had to be something pertaining to the military and not to *us*. Surprisingly, that annoyed me a little… very little.

Claudius Saint-Olliare was a *young* general. He'd been married once, or so the stories go. He'd been a bachelor my entire military career of eight years, and for the last few years of it, we'd been on and off. Now, we're off completely because we'd almost gotten caught together more than once. Our relationship was a big military *no-no* because of the difference in our ranks. So, we decided to call it quits on my twenty-fifth birthday. I was promoted, and stationed at a different armory from him, and I met my current boyfriend, Jensen Lyons, at a post office.

My phone began buzzing in my hand again. Ollie.

I picked up and cleared my throat. "General St. Olliare, is everything alright?"

2

The silence on the airwaves forced me to take a deep breath.

"It's bad, Keoni."

Tucking my phone between my ear and shoulder, I grabbed my toothbrush and began my day at two in the morning.

"I need you to get to the joint force headquarters as soon as possible," Ollie said.

"Sir," I paused to spit out a glob of toothpaste, "may I ask for more details?"

He sighed. "China has invaded Taiwan."

I froze. The water raced to the drain as I lowered my toothbrush.

"I need you, Keoni."

"Sir—"

"For the team I'm putting together," he spoke over me. "Your tactical expertise is needed right now, and you will be working in dual positions."

"What do you mean?"

"I mean, we're going to promote you to major for this operation. If you prove yourself, when all this is over, you'll remain as a major, or maybe even get another promotion. But you'll still be expected to train soldiers. You're one of the most valuable soldiers we've got right now, and you've made more like you—"

I grunted and he stopped for a second.

"Well," he chuckled, "not *quite* like you."

"Thank you, sir, for the promotion." I tried to sound professional. Tried to remind him that a small country had just been invaded and this was not the time to flirt. Plus … I was with Jensen now. Jensen who was still asleep and didn't care who I spoke to at 2 in the morning. Jensen who won't question me about this phone call later because he trusts me that much.

Ollie grunted into the silence, regaining my attention. "You can thank me when you get here, captain."

"Of course," I said slowly.

"Further details will follow upon your arrival. Come straight to my office."

"Roger."

He hung up without saying anything else. It took me an extra moment to register everything he'd just said. I'm getting promoted. But, more importantly, China just invaded Taiwan.

I finished cleaning up and grabbed a uniform from the closet. The blankets shifted when I crept through the bedroom to dig through my drawers for an undershirt. Jensen was turning over in bed, watching me silently as I moved around the room.

"What's going on, Ki?"

"They called me in. It's not good." I pulled my shirt on and tucked it in.

"Can you tell me?"

"Not yet. But you'll know everything by morning."

"Ok," he said quietly.

Jensen had been good to me. Never pushy or forceful, he always listened and accepted whatever I told him. I liked that

4

about Jensen, his easygoingness. We hardly argued because of it, and he loved the military as much as I did. He supported me, and I have enjoyed every second of our lives together. It was different being with someone, and not looking over your shoulder. Not scheduling meet up spots or a secret rendezvous. With Ollie being my superior, we've never been able to have the kind of relationship either of us wanted, and that drove a wedge between us. A yearlong wedge.

"I'll probably be gone for a while," I said to Jensen. "But I'll call you. Make sure you get my uniforms from the cleaners and have them for me by the evening in case I get some free time to come home."

"It's that serious?" he asked as he clicked on a lamp sitting on the bedside table.

"Yeah." I blinked at the sudden intrusion of light. "But I'm getting a promotion out of it, so that's good."

He laughed as he pulled on his glasses. "That just means I won't see you for the next month."

"I promise I'll make time for you." I crossed the room and leaned over the bed for a kiss. "Besides," I said as I caressed his somber face, "our one-year anniversary is tomorrow. I'll definitely make time for that."

"Good." He was smiling now, though I knew the distance would bother him every day I wasn't sleeping beside him. "I don't want to celebrate alone."

I kissed him once more before placing my cap on and taking my leave.

Seven years ago, Russia invaded Ukraine. This emboldened China with their plans to invade Taiwan. But it never happened. Tensions rose to a boiling point in a three-way conflict between the United States, China, and Taiwan. But, like any good chef—when the water's overboiling, you turn it off. But … in a three-way battle, who was really the head chef? Who called the shots?

Tensions died down when Russia completely annexed Ukraine. They built a giant wall around the Ukrainian border and a dome over various regions and cities. And then Russia went dead quiet. They cut themselves off from the world. Resources, weapons, everything imaginable, Russia stopped importing and exporting.

It took several stealth drones to get information on Ukraine. Russia was taking drones out regularly and keeping the public's eyes off them. The last thing one of our drones picked up was Chinese officials visiting Russians in Ukrainian conquered territory. It left a bad taste in the world's mouth, but we were able to swallow it when we needed to.

When Taiwan and China stopped feuding, so did the US, and for the last five years, the world has been at peace. A famine came, but it was quickly chased down by China's kindness to the world, which made us forget about their secret meetings with the Russians. They strengthened their ties around the globe, sending food and water everywhere they could. They even helped more countries than the US.

In fact, China helped the US.

When there was a chip shortage in the middle of the famine, the US had turned to Taiwan, but they came up short. Israel offered the components needed to craft more chips and China stepped in and offered their services to build the chips. Of course, the US agreed. In exchange for their services, the US sent weapons and boats. It was all we had to offer, though it was silly since we were all at peace.

There've been no signs of agitation, no rising tension between China and anyone else. They've been on good terms with the entire world. Back when Russia invaded Ukraine, China had taken over a few villages in Nepal, claiming they belonged to Tibet, which China conquered long ago. It was a bloody encounter. However, when the famine hit, the rest of Nepal and parts of India surrendered to China's leadership, which expanded Chinese territory further than ever before. We weren't worried, though, since the US and China were friendly now.

China had even found a way to work out the border conflicts with Myanmar. That was a show of good will that China was willing to work with anyone since the border of Myanmar edged forty percent of the world's population. China claimed the terrorist groups who'd been at the border (and had ties to Hezbollah and Hamas after China signed a treaty with the Islamic Brotherhood) weren't of their control, and the brotherhood had turned on them. They got rid of the terrorists and peace was bestowed upon the earth.

So why now?

Why, out of nowhere, has China attacked Taiwan? After all they've done, all the resources they've given. Why?

I couldn't figure it out as I drove to the joint force headquarters. All I knew right then was that Taiwan, our ally, was in trouble. The USA had remained suspicious of China until the famine hit. China's global contributions softened the US, and we'd been working up a policy to keep the peace between the US and China, and in the Asian-Pacific region with China owning so much more territory now.

Pulling into the parking lot, I realized there were only a few cars here. I figured everyone was on their way, and that there probably wouldn't be too many people in on this. This was going to be a big operation, but knowing the current military leadership, we'll be trying our hardest not to send in so many soldiers.

Ollie met me at the entrance. Tall and strong, looking particularly powerful today in his crisp military uniform. The early sunlight winked off the pins on his shoulders.

"Morning." He nodded.

"Morning, sir." I saluted him, which made him laugh and throw a hand at me.

"Calm down." He chuckled, and the sound made me immediately blush. "It's just us right now. The official meeting won't start for another thirty minutes to an hour. I've got some guys making calls now."

I lowered my hand and squinted at Ollie. He'd always been handsome. Green eyes against his warm ivory skin and dark hair made everyone give him a second glance. You'd never look at Brigadier General Claudius St. Olliare and think he was turning forty this year.

"It's been a while, captain," Ollie said as he nodded for me to follow him.

"Sir—"

"Keoni," he did an about-face—literally—and stopped me in my tracks. "When it's just the two of us, call me Ollie. Like you used to." He paused. "That's an order."

"Understood." He lifted a brow, and I sighed. "Understood, *Ollie*."

"Good. I'll brief you in my office."

We walked in silence, and I realized I didn't have much left in the tank to keep up the professional act. I hadn't seen Ollie in a year. My promotion to captain had been his parting gift. He put me in for it early since I technically qualified and we needed the space.

I'd gone into the Army National Guard as an enlisted soldier and met Ollie. I was going to college at the time, and he caught me studying on the job one day when he crossed into the Guard's part of the armory. I was totally smitten by him, though he was scolding me, *and* there was an age (and rank) difference which I found out much later into our relationship. My studying on the job became a joke between the two of us, and after a while, we started seeing each other.

He was tutoring me after work in his office, when the armory was supposed to be closed. I enjoyed the tutoring so much that instead of quitting school completely when it got too hard, I only took a break to come back to it later. That helped me when I switched over to active duty at Ollie's wish. But when we almost got caught together the second time, I didn't want to see him anymore.

Our jobs were at risk, and though my feelings for Ollie were strong, I had begun to love the military more than him. Especially after the armed forces had made several exceptions for me.

At the time, I was a first lieutenant. I'd been enrolled as an officer when I went active duty and started higher than my colleagues since I'd spent time enlisted. As a parting gift from Ollie, he put my name forward for the captain rank early, and I got it. I never thanked him because I didn't know how without deciding against my career to stay by his side.

"Captain Banks, have a seat," he said as we entered his office. It was a large room, but it was mostly empty. A few pictures of him on the wall as he moved through the ranks, a large oak desk with military coins and other sentiments on it as decorations.

"I thought you said not to be formal."

He smiled. "KiKi, darling, if you wanted me to call you by your pet name, all you had to do was say so."

"Ollie, I'm seeing someone else," I said as I sat.

He rolled his eyes and closed the office door. "A year later and you're still taking care of that loser, Johnson?"

"Jensen," I corrected. "And I'm not *taking care of him*. Jensen is a tax accountant. He makes good money."

"He sits in an office all day." Ollie's words left his mouth before he realized them as he took a seat in a big comfy office chair.

I raised a brow and glanced around. "I don't see a difference."

He scoffed. "You know what I mean."

Suppressing a chuckle, I asked, "Is there any reason you called me in so early?"

"Well, I've got to pin you, and I've got to brief you."

"Pin me?" He lifted a bag of patches. "You know? Change your rank or whatever."

"Oh." I glanced down at my sandy brown boots. "I forgot."

"You're not allowed to forget anything else once I put this patch on you," he said as he stood from the desk. "It's serious, Keoni, more serious than we initially thought."

"Just tell me."

"China invaded Taiwan, which we thought was just an attack. But recently, we've gotten an update that there's been movement in Russia and the Russia-Ukraine territory."

"What kind of movement?"

"Ships. A full naval fleet. We suspect they're carrying tanks."

I scratched my head. "I don't understand. Why is Russia on the move now? And where are they going?"

"That's the part that makes this so bad for us." He glanced down at the map on his desk. It was beneath a glass frame, keeping the old thing in tip top shape. "They're using

Ukrainian ships that were ported in Turkey. But the fleet isn't in the Black Sea. They're moving through the Mediterranean Sea."

I held my breath, hoping he wouldn't say what I thought was coming next.

"We think they're going for our oldest ally. We think they're aimed at Israel."

2

The People Who Have Gathered Livestock and Goods

Keoni

"Everyone, this is Major Keoni Banks. She'll be part of my team," Ollie said as we all stood around the table.

I nodded at the introduction. A few wrinkly old men nodded back. These were some of the most powerful men in the United States Army. It was an honor to be here, though I didn't get to relish that for long. Some of the wrinkled faces held scowls, while the younger ones had raised brows. I knew before walking in that there would be opposition to my presence, however, the wave of dislike was stronger than I'd expected, which made me want to shrink away.

Ollie, on the other hand, wasn't bothered. He continued to speak, turning, and acknowledging the entire table as he said, "Major Banks is here today as my trusted assistant. I need her ears for this meeting so please don't hold back."

"I've never seen or heard of Major Banks," a rigid old man with pale skin frowned at me.

I inclined my head and chose not to reply. I knew my place at the table was just to absorb everything said and bring it back to Ollie's office. I was just a fly on the wall. However, that didn't make this experience any easier.

You're a soldier, I reminded myself. I'd survived brutal training and dangerous missions. Dealing with a little dislike shouldn't make me so uncomfortable. It was just that I felt like everyone knew about my complicated—and unprofessional— history with Ollie. It felt like all the scowls and raised brows were acts of judgement for my past, not the present.

"General Jacobs," Ollie said dryly, "Lieutenant General Murphy asked me to fill the Major vacancy on the squad with my own choosing. Major Banks was the top captain in her class. She was in charge of over two hundred soldiers and has taught excellent training classes over the past year at our combat facilities. Her skillset and tactical abilities set her aside from the rest of her comrades. She's been—"

"Alright," Jacobs fanned the air in dismissal.

Ollie held in his smug smile, exchanging it for a courteous nod. He was just weighing Jacobs down with information, but it was nice to hear my rap sheet regarded with such esteem in a room full of full bird colonels and two-, three-, and four-star generals.

"Can we begin now?" the four-star general asked.

"Sorry, sir," Jacobs apologized.

General Collins waved a hand and we all sat down.

14

"Let's lay it all on the table. What do we know?" Collins asked.

Colonel Jones, a big brown-skinned man said, "To start, sir, China has invaded Taiwan after five years of peace."

"Do we have a 'why' yet?"

"No, we don't have a 'why' for anything, but the pieces of the puzzle are coming together."

"How so?"

Lieutenant Colonel Whitney raised her hand, and I could see the clear gloss on her nails a mile away. "Thus far, we know China is invading Taiwan via naval forces and ground forces. What has been reported to us is that the artillery being used, and the naval ships rolling into the Taiwan Strait belong to different branches of the US military."

Collins glared at Whitney as if she was the one driving the Naval ships. "What are you saying? That they're framing us?"

"No, sir, they're just using our ships to win this fight."

"It's a clear warning to us," Jacobs added. "If we try to join the fight, we've got nothing on these guys because they're using our own weapons. It'll be like the US fighting itself."

"Correct," Ollie said beside me. "I got a report that mentioned Nepalian forces are bringing their US weapons to the fight as well."

"Which just means they've got enough resources to at least threaten us, privately or publicly," Collins said. He looked distraught as he rocked in his chair at the head of the long brown table. The room was tense, but not because we were emotional, we were short on information, and we knew Collins didn't like that.

Rustling his hand through his red wavy hair, he said, "If they're using all the weapons we've sent Nepal in this invasion, China gets to start out ahead of us *because* they're using *our* weapons. They've got the extra manpower from Nepal and India if they need it." He scratched the tiny bit of red stubble peppering his jaw. We were called here through the night, I suspected he didn't have time to shave.

"This could be troubling if China calls on all their allies. We've sent weapons all over," Whitney spoke.

"I don't think they'll need all their allies," Collins said. "But it does beg the question; if they've been using this time of peace for war plans against Taiwan… does that mean China's help during the famine is going to come at an even greater cost in the future? This is just Taiwan, what if they want to invade the rest of India? They've got ties with the entire Middle East."

"Their territory would take up at least forty percent of the world if they grab India, maybe more." Jacobs added.

"But that's just China, sir." Hack, a younger man and another lieutenant colonel, raised his pencil and continued. "Russia has seen movement too. Aircrafts and ships have been moving towards Israel since ten last night our time."

"Hold on." Collins lifted a hand weakly. "China is invading Taiwan at the same time Russia, after years of silence, is moving in on Israel—and we don't have a 'why' yet?"

"The only thing we suspect is that Russia is low on resources, and Israel is still the Land of Milk and Honey.

16

They've got a little of everything and aren't running short," Colonel Jones suggested. "Russia may be heading there for their resources."

"But why on the same night?"

"Because they're forcing us to pick a side," Ollie spoke up again. "Israel is our oldest ally, but we vowed to help Taiwan too."

"That was years ago," Jacobs said roughly.

"So we abandon Taiwan because that was years ago?" General Murphy, who hadn't spoken this entire time, finally joined in. "Does anyone else think that's nuts? Seriously, we vowed to help Israel long ago too. What reason do we have to stick to that besides time if that's all we're basing things off?"

"Don't make it personal or emotional," Jacobs hissed. "We've got to do what's best for the country, not what'll make us sleep at night."

"There won't be much of that anyway," Ollie said as he sat back in his chair.

"General St. Olliare, care to leave the sarcastic comments at home when there are serious problems on the rise?" General Collins snapped.

"Sorry, sir. Roger, sir."

"Thank you." Collins glanced over and jutted his chin toward me. "St. Olliare says you're good. You run day to day operations for soldiers. What's your take on everything?"

I paused, almost shocked that he'd spoken to me.

Ollie turned in his chair with a raised brow, and I glanced away from him back at our four-star general who was demanding an answer.

"Well, sir, our ties link back to Israel and Taiwan. We have to look at what we gain, and what we're willing to send. Everyone will be expecting our help. Either we figure out a way to help both, which is impossible since we just don't have the men and resources to spare. Or we pick one based on the supplies they give us."

"What a stupid answer," General Murphy snapped at me. He was a big, tall man, greying brown locks and face that looked like he used to be a doll. I only nodded at his response. I was the lowest ranking officer present with only two tours under my belt and eight years of service. These guys had more experience than me and understood this world far better than I did. I was supposed to be a fly, and so I tried my hardest to ignore his brashness.

"We can't pick both, and we can't just pick one," Murphy said.

"*That* was an actual stupid answer," Collins frowned. "You didn't offer any solutions, not like Major Banks. Her answer wasn't stupid, it was actually a step in the right direction."

"Thank you, sir."

"If we're stepping in this direction," Lt. Colonel Hack chimed in, "then, sir, we've got to look at the bigger picture. Who's going to require the most help? If our resources are scarce, and Israel's aren't, then we should focus our efforts on Taiwan who's got even less than us."

"Or not," Whitney said. Her brick orange hair was pulled back in the tightest bun possible. I thought she was pretty, and Ollie did too, apparently. They've had interactions, but that's not my business. I didn't need to be thinking about the past anyway with so much on the table right now.

"If Taiwan needs the most help, and we're short, let's help the guys who barely need our help. And then maybe they'll send us more resources."

"And maybe not," Murphy spat.

"I don't see why they wouldn't. Israel has always helped us," Whitney explained.

"Taiwan is a small island that is going to be surrounded by morning. How can we leave them to fight for themselves?"

"If they're going to be surrounded by morning, then there's nothing we can do. Why jump into a fight that's already got a sure outcome?" General Jacobs tossed his hands open. "Going into Taiwan will cost us soldiers, and weapons. Which we've been short on both since the famine. We didn't have enough money in the budget for weapon updates, and we lost a lot of people when they found out military affiliation did not entitle them to bigger or better rations than everyone else." Jacobs looked downtrodden. His eyes were hazed with emotion as he said quietly, "When I was a boy, patriotism was alive and healthy. We ran at every problem with such force, the momentum after the collision kept us going for decades. Now, things are much different."

"I've seen too many body bags for my own liking." The depth of Colonel Jones' voice filled the entire room. "I think

19

we should consider how many more lives it'll cost us. Which fight will cost us the least amount of lives? Don't worry about weapons because the budget will be readjusted to compensate for sending help. But bodies, *soldiers*, they can't be replaced."

"And not just because people are irreplaceable." Ollie shrugged. "Like Jacobs said, there aren't enough willing participants. We'll have to have a draft to recruit people. And then our entire country will really hate us, and the world will know how weak we are."

"You're right." Whitney nodded. "If people get wind that we're weak, or don't have enough soldiers, it won't be good for us."

"Alright so what's the solution? Discussing this over and over isn't going to get us anywhere." General Jacobs said.

Collins tapped his finger on the table for a moment. "If we're going to help one, we have to help them both."

"But, sir——" Murphy began but the general raised his hand and silenced him.

"Our ties to Israel are too deep. Giving them up to fight alone would be treacherous. But Taiwan is small and certainly needs our help."

"Sir, we can't afford to help both," Hack said softly as he adjusted his glasses.

"We have no choice," Collins said. He looked up at Ollie. "Get a plan to me in the next twelve hours, so that I can be in a room with the rest of the forces in the next thirteen hours."

"Roger," Ollie said as we all stood.

Collins dismissed us, and Ollie and I made a beeline for his office.

"Close the door," he said as he hunched over his desk. He remained right there even as I turned and quietly shut the door. His eyes were glued to the map beneath the glass. "We've got men stationed on Luzon Island in the Philippines," he said quietly, as if talking to himself. Then, in a louder tone, he added, "We can send half of those soldiers by air and get them there in an hour. The only problem is that it would probably take a full twenty-four hours to get one of our naval ships making its routes through the Philippines sea there with enough weapons and ammo to last until the next ship arrived."

"How long would that be?" I asked as I walked over to the desk.

"Probably another three days if we want to stay undiscovered. If we're just going to bring a fleet, two days at top speed."

"Is this really a good idea? Sending soldiers over there when we know they may not make it back? It's a done deal for Taiwan."

"I know," his voice was low and serious as his eyes studied the map. It's been an entire year, but I could never forget Ollie's passion for the military. It's where my love for the Army came from. He always spoke so proudly of the US armed forces. He said it was the best job he'd ever had, and I believed that.

"All I can do is spare the lives I can for now. We'll send air support to Israel just to scope out what exactly is

21

happening. I'll get one of the guys on the team to get this information formatted and get the files back to Collins."

"And then what?"

"Our plans are just a starting point, really. Collins will get this information to the Secretary of Defense in Washington."

"I see."

In the silence, the weight of how serious the situation was began to drag me down. I'd been given top secret clearance on a matter that was way above my paygrade, and all I could do was offer meager input.

"Hey…" Ollie placed his hand on mine, as if he'd read my thoughts. "Decisions must be made, sweetheart. I need you to be strong. It's going to get a lot worse before it gets any better."

"I know," I whispered. "I just wish it didn't have to be this way."

Ollie walked around the desk, taking my hand in his and turning me to face him. We'd been busy all morning. He briefed me, and then we were stuck in a meeting until now. We hadn't had the chance to catch up, and I didn't even know if I wanted to. Keeping things professional had always been something neither of us were good at. But there was so much more going on than us. And I've got a boyfriend. I didn't want to be focused on Ollie… yet I was.

I found myself unable to pull from his mesmerizing gaze. All thoughts of China, Taiwan, soldiers, and even Jensen were out the window as Ollie stepped a little closer.

"It's been too long, Keoni."

"Don't do that. Not right now."

22

He pulled me forward, slipping a hand to the small of my back. "The five years of peace was just shattered." I tried to fight. "The world is in chaos."

"It is, and all I want to do is steal a kiss from you." Caressing my cheek, his eyes were locked with mine. We were sealed in that moment, and there was no going back.

"I've missed you, Keoni."

There was no reason for me to respond because the exchange between us was enough to relay the feelings I've buried, but never truly gotten rid of.

The brigadier general was a liar. The passion that filled the room between us was not stolen by him, it was owed to him, and I had every desire to pay him in full.

3

Go Up Against the Land of Unwalled Villages

Zion

My father, Pastor Jillian Reinhardt—a German man with a powerful voice, and a heart for God—named me the deacon of his megachurch, The City on a Hill, when I was just twenty-one. That was seven years ago when I was truly walking with God. When I had a heart for Him the same way my father did.

Back then, I loved God. I honored God. I was on fire for God.

There is still some small part of me that feels that way. It's just … very small now. I know I still have at least some respect for God because of the constant guilt that swirls in my gut every time a 'sister' from church becomes a lover. One of *many* lovers.

Go ahead, judge me. I judge myself every day.

I want to do the right thing, I really do. But believing in God went out the door when I ran into a woman just one year after becoming a deacon. Her name was Allison Reed. She's long gone by now, but Ally was a walking firecracker. She had slim legs, and round hips, with wild curls that drove me mad.

We used to sneak off after services, hiding in the back of the church's book center. It was in the far corner, near the history books, that I gave her my virginity one evening. Dad had entrusted me with the key to lock the store up at night, and she was there, and so was all the tension between us. The next thing I knew, I was seeing her regularly, but just for hookups. I couldn't get enough of her.

Allison Reed soon left the church after a visit from an up-and-coming pastor. We'd held a convention, and she caught his eye. The two were married a year later, and then welcomed their first child just last year. But my heart wasn't broken for long. Ally was my first, but she definitely wasn't my last. Though, if she had been, I'd be a totally different man from who I am today. I'm a pitiful shame, and I know this. But women … there's something about them that I can't get enough of. One is not enough. No way.

I threw the blankets back, and saw Jala Verde, or rather, Sister Verde, beneath the blankets snoring away. She had every right to snore from exhaustion after last night. But it was Sunday morning, and I needed enough time to get my head straight and 'filled' before service.

Trust me, I hated it as much as anyone else. But I didn't know how to go back to God with the whole world in my hand.

I had everything I wanted. Money, women, sex. Going back to God meant giving that up. I wasn't ready to do that.

"Jala," I called flatly as I sat on the edge of the bed. Picking her clothes from mine, I threw them on her, and she grunted awake. "Get up. It's five. You need to be gone in ten minutes before anyone sees you."

She huffed deeply. "Let's skip today. You don't even need to be there."

"It's my job to be there and like it or not, that church is my father's legacy. *My* legacy at some point. I've got to be there."

"Since when did you care about God or a legacy that has to do with Him?" She snorted as I heard her sitting up. "I like it better when you're the Zion from last night." Her bare flat chest was against my back as she threw her arms around my neck.

"Jala," I patted her hand, "get out."

She scoffed in my ear, her hands slowly unfolding as I stood and headed for the bathroom.

— ÷ —

"God made it clear," my father spoke as he marched across the pulpit, "that there's redemption for everybody. Even the greatest of sinners. You all remember Paul."

He was going on about Paul's encounter with Jesus, and how he'd been changed forever.

"Some of you must be knocked off your horse to come to your senses. And it's not going to be a literal knocking off of a horse."

The crowd of thousands began to laugh along with him, his throaty chuckle echoed through the microphone like a harmony to their amusement. He smiled as he glanced back at me. I gave him an approving nod, before he looked over at my mother, Rhoda Reinhardt. My mother had influenced my taste in women. She was the most beautiful woman I'd ever seen. Dimpled cheeks, round eyes, and the smoothest nutbrown skin in all of Missouri.

The women I went after didn't exactly look or act like my mother—that'd be weird. But they always shared her complexion. Like Jala, who was crossing her legs on the front pew in a skirt that was arguably too short for church, and definitely too short for the front bench where I had a clear view of her shapely calves. I knew she'd done it on purpose, but no one else knew.

From time to time, Jala would tug on the little shawl across her lap, sliding it off to give me a peep show of her legs while I sat in the pulpit. She would wave her shawl around like she was so into the sermon, before crossing one slender leg over the other, and eyeing me as she finally put the shawl back.

Jala knew how to work me. She was almost as good as Ally back in the day. However, when I was with Ally, I was a young stupid kid. Fresh in the deacon position, I'd let that go to my head and got a little prideful. A beautiful woman threw herself at me and I caught her and hung on as long as I could.

It was wrong back then, and I knew it was wrong now. I knew it would never be right. But Jala was good at making me forget the guilt. She was good at keeping me distracted during service and keeping me busy afterwards. I enjoyed letting her eat away at my guilt, though my father, bless his unsuspecting soul, always managed to stir the pot of guilt with his sermons.

"Paul killed the very people Jesus died for," he went on, making me sweat. "And God forgave him. You, my friends, can be forgiven. There's nothing you can do, no river you can cross that'll keep you separated from the love of God. He wants to redeem you. Dust you off and make you shine bright again."

His words were piercing, and the gentleness with which he spoke made me want to crawl into a ball and weep for God's mercy. I wanted to change, wanted to be better, but Jala...

I glanced up at her. Her shawl was off, and she was standing now, allowing me to get a good look at her in that tight blue dress. It took everything in me not to walk down the stage and take her away right there in front of everyone. But Jala was a distraction, and I knew it.

My father had gone on, asking us to raise our hands to receive redemption. I followed along, setting an example to the congregation. They looked like a sea, the way they all blended together against the blue sanctuary. Blue walls and a vast blue carpet that rolled all the way up the stage. The chairs were all an eggshell white. It was my mother's design. She loved blue, but she said too much would make the sanctuary look small, even though there was floor seating, and balcony seating. I didn't press the issue, considering I was only fifteen when we first built this sanctuary.

I was born into Christianity. Believing in Jesus and accepting His sacrifice. It was all good, but sometimes I felt like I never really got the chance to believe on my own. I felt like I believed because I was supposed to. Because I'd been raised to. Because there had never been any other choice for me.

That was still no excuse for my behavior. I could've challenged that feeling by getting to know Christ for myself, but that didn't happen.

"Psst!"

I glanced around. My father was still walking across the front of the stage in a mint green suit and white shirt, while my mother and the rest of the church council stood and worshipped or prayed. Giving my attention back to my father, I heard my name called.

God? I thought. *Are You calling me? Am I actually hearing Your voice?*

I was frightened now. God had called to me, and there was a swelling fear in my stomach that made me feel sick. Maybe today would be the day I was knocked off my horse.

"Zion!" the whisper came again, and just as I began to give in, hoping that the voice was of God, the voice called out, "Back here!"

I looked over my shoulder immediately. It was Tony. A thin dark-skinned guy with an afro stood in the curtains of the stage, waving a piece of paper at me. Looking over at my

29

mother, I waited until I got her attention. With a firm nod, she gave me permission to go backstage.

I took quick steps, trying not to draw too much attention to myself. When I was out of view, I ripped the curtains back in heartbreak and fury, snapping at Tony, "What could you possibly want!?"

He cowered a little, a confused look on his face.

I sighed. "Sorry. Rough morning."

"You alright?"

"Yeah. What did you want?"

"Well, I don't know if I should tell you now since you're so upset."

I didn't want to tell him I was *this* close to giving my heart back to God, that for the first time in so long I actually felt like God was calling me. But he'd interrupted. Despite Tony's voice being the one in reality, I knew I'd heard the voice of God when I was standing there. It was clear and calm. There was no mistaking His voice. It almost felt like more than God calling me, it was like He *wanted* me.

Maybe I was wrong.

Why'd He want me now? I'd been doing what I wanted, who'd want a dirty temple? I criticized myself in my mind before noticing the awkward silence between Tony and me.

"You already interrupted service, just tell me what it is," I ordered.

"I was interrupting because there's a phone call for your father from the president."

"Of what? And why on a Sunday?"

He shook his head, the thick fro' staying in place. "No. The President of the United States of America wants to talk to your father."

I blinked. "For what?"

My dad had met with the president on multiple occasions. Giving him council on political issues and pushing for the Biblical agenda to be accepted in the nation.

President Warrick Fallon and my father had become friends by pure accident. At a political campaign, before Fallon was president, my father challenged him on his argument for the removal of educational religious institutions below the collegiate level. President Fallon believed that children were being groomed by Christian parents. He believed their ideals were brainwashing and dangerous, suffocating the founding principle of freedom. Freedom to live as children wanted to live without the restrictions of overbearing religion.

My father told him otherwise.

Pastor Reinhardt boldly explained that freedom belonged to America because we stood for Christ who was the freer of all people. It only made sense to learn about the One who brought freedom to all. It goes without saying that the president lost that debate.

"President Fallon said it was urgent," Tony said. "Something about the end of world peace."

"The end of world peace? This came from the president himself?"

"No." He waved a hand. "His secretary or whatever."

"Oh. Well, I can't interrupt my father. Service will be over soon. Tell him to call back."

"When world peace just ended?"

I shrugged. "What am I supposed to do? Run out there and tell my dad, the congregation, *and* God to hold their horses, we've got bigger problems?"

He sighed. "Can you at least speak to her?"

"Me? No. I've got to get back."

His brows came together quickly as he reached out and grabbed my arm. "Please, Zion!"

"What are you so scared of?" I snapped as I ripped my arm free from him. "And lower your voice."

"The president is spooked enough to call your dad about *world peace*. Something's going on. Aren't you even the slightest bit interested?"

Rubbing a hand over my face, I gave in.

"Fine. Whatever."

I followed Tony to the office section of the church facility, entering my father's office. The grey phone on his sleek desk had a red light blinking on line one.

Tony stood there, nervously wringing his hands.

I grunted, "Get out, you're making me nervous."

He tossed his hands up and walked out the door, pulling it shut gently behind himself.

"Let's get this over with," I mumbled, picking up the phone and hitting the first line. "This is Zion Reinhardt, my father, Jillian Reinhardt, is still in service. He's unavailable right now."

32

"That's alright. Would you relay a private message to him?" The woman's voice was clear, but old.

"Sure, I've got a pen and paper."

"You won't need it."

I lowered the pad slowly as fear crept into my mind. I looked around the room in the silence as I realized that whatever happened must've been incredibly devastating. Though these four walls were not crumbling as I sat on my father's desk, someone else's walls must've been for the private message to be so memorable that pen and paper weren't needed.

I tried to swallow, but my mouth felt as dry as a cotton ball as I searched for her voice. When it came, I wished I hadn't searched for it. I wished I could have *un*heard what she'd said.

"China has invaded Taiwan." The woman paused.

I gulped.

"And after five years of peace and solidarity, there's been reported movement from the Russia-Ukraine territory. We believe warships are coursed for Israel."

She was right. That information *was* unforgettable.

4

After Many Days, You Will Be Mustered

Keoni

I checked my phone, reading over the apology I'd sent to Jensen four days ago for missing our anniversary. I hadn't planned on missing it. Honestly. But I've been caught up at the office and caught up with Ollie. It's like the fire we've always shared with each other had been suppressed for a year. And now with its newfound freedom within the four walls of Ollie's office, it's back with a vengeance.

Lying on the couch, I scrolled to read Jensen's thoughtful reply again to sop up my guilt, then the door opened, and Ollie stepped inside.

"I thought you'd be hard at work?" he said as he passed me a sandwich.

I closed my phone and pushed all thoughts of Jensen out of my head. "I'm tired of working," I said as I took the sandwich and made room for him on the cushiony couch.

"No, you're tired of doing *office* work."

"It doesn't seem right." I stared at the wrapping on the sandwich. It was some kind of ham sandwich on a big bun. The cling wrap had gathered in one spot on the back of the sandwich, and I traced the wrinkly lines as Ollie began to munch on his own. They were clearly rations, something we'd finally gotten good at.

The American economy had a brutal wakeup call when the famine hit. We were in debt to so many people, with little to offer them in return. And the famine did nothing for our debt or favors owed except rack them up. We'd crippled ourselves from all the outsourcing, and maintaining a focus on popularity, instead of humanitarian issues like the growing slums. There were far too many of them after the first wave of a virus that took lives within hours ten years ago.

The mutations and variations of that virus wrecked America first and then the rest of the world, along with the old sicknesses reemerging from the melting glaciers. America the Beautiful had lost most of her beauty by the time the famine rolled around.

When the famine ended, she was flat out ugly. And stressed with unkempt hair and torn clothes.

"You're a true soldier, aren't you?" Ollie said around his food.

"What do you mean?" I pulled my gaze from the sandwich.

"You're sitting here thinking about how unfair it is to be here and not on the ground with your fellow comrades, right?" He bumped his shoulder against mine. "You know any one of those guys would give anything to take your place here where it's safe?"

"And you know I'd trade with them in an instant."

Ollie swallowed the last bit of his sandwich before taking mine and opening it. "How many tours have you done?"

"You know I did two," I grunted. "I was sent to Africa to help train their military forces, and I was part of a specialist team that did a stealth mission to rescue some Americans from the Ukraine before Russia completely took over."

He was looking at me now as he took a bite out of my sandwich. With full cheeks, his green eyes grazed over me until they focused on the patch sitting on my leg. "You earned a purple heart for that mission, didn't you?"

I didn't speak.

"I still remember when you returned. I couldn't see you for thirty-three hours while they did what they could on you. Your eye might've been saved if you'd come home early."

"That wasn't possible."

"Sure, it was. You just wouldn't leave the mission. The call to abort the mission with immediate return was approved, but you wouldn't come home, even *after* I begged you."

The halting silence brought back vivid memories from that mission. The mission that almost ended my career because of my injury. Thankfully, I've always excelled as a soldier, physically and mentally, and I won my case to be allowed to remain active duty and not forced into medical retirement.

Our group was on the move when we drove over an improvised explosive device during the mission. We scrambled out the trucks and tanks to get to safety with the civilians, but we were surrounded. I lost my eye defending a civilian who tried to make a run for it. He darted out, but thankfully I was on the enemy before he fired the gun. After I knocked the weapon away, we were engaged in hand-to-hand combat until he pulled a knife. He cut me across the face, leaving me sightless in one eye, and a permanent gash along the side of my head.

I won the battle, without part of my vision. We held our own until backup showed up, and I was treated as best as possible in the back of a car when headquarters were called. Ollie was able to get in on the line and pleaded with me to come home. But I refused. That was the last thing I remembered before passing out.

I was out cold for over two days as my eye had gotten infected from the bandages. When we returned, I was sent in for immediate operation, and many attempts were made, but half my vision was gone. All that was left was a faded iris, and scars that I'll live with forever.

I grabbed my patch and put it over my right eye.

"You always look so strong with your patch," Ollie said as he reached up and placed a hand to my cheek. "But I prefer you to keep it off when it's just us."

Claudius had never stopped calling me beautiful after I lost my eye. The day after I was released from the hospital, he came to visit me in the recovery center to 'pay his respects.'

Despite all the bandages and face wraps, Ollie told me I was still the most beautiful woman he'd ever known. The night I received my purple heart was the first time we were intimate since I'd lost my eye. Most people didn't live to receive such an award, but I had.

Ollie was quick to sweep me off my feet and carry me into a hotel room much later after the ceremony. He kissed me like nothing had changed about me, clung to me like he'd die because I was the only one who could keep him together. But none of that compared to the moment he pulled my patch off and kissed every scar and gash.

A knock came to the door, and I gave Claudius a tightlipped smile. "I guess I better keep it on."

He rolled his eyes and leaned over to kiss my cheek. "You better act like a soldier and not my hot younger girlfriend." Trading my cheek for neck, Claudius kissed me again and then headed for the door.

Ollie and I had never made things official between us. We weren't even exclusive—because we couldn't be—but we always came back to each other after a few weeks or so. We'd argue over something stupid, and Ollie would try to make me jealous by going out with women totally different from me. I never let it bother me, though, because he always came back.

Standing from the couch, I tried to push the girly thoughts of being Ollie's girlfriend away because I was *Jensen's* girlfriend.

I hardened my gaze on the paperwork on his desk as the door opened.

Captain Luther stood there holding a folder. He questioned my presence with a single look, but I outranked him, and the look was all that passed between us before his focus fell back to Ollie.

"Sir," he stood at attention until Ollie said, "At ease, captain. What is it?"

"There's news, sir, a threat has been issued to the United States by China."

Ollie nodded, and the ruddy captain went on. "Russia's ships haven't moved. But we just received word that Sudanese ships are headed for the Gulf of Aqaba."

Ollie looked over his shoulder at me, a grim expression capturing his features before turning back to the captain. "Anything else?"

"There will be a meeting in an hour. Representatives from each branch will be there."

"The Guard too?"

"Yes, sir."

"Why?"

"I was told they were coming because of the public outcry. Crowd control is needed."

Ollie took a deep breath to keep from rolling his eyes. He didn't like the Guard, said they were paper boys. I had no ill feelings towards them, not just because I'd been one of them, but because they went through basic training like the rest of us.

They were tough guys, despite the part-time, paper pushing jobs.

"Alright, captain, come back in forty-five minutes for us and—"

"They're asking that you attend alone, sir."

The air went rigid at Luther's words, and I knew Ollie was going to snap. I set down the papers I'd been distracting myself with and walked over to squeeze myself beside Ollie in the doorway. His vision snapped to mine; anger written all over his handsome face.

"I'll have the Brigadier General ready for the meeting," I told Luther. "Briefed with ideas, and solutions based on the knowledge we have."

"Of course, Major Banks." Captain Luther gave me a polite nod before nodding at Ollie too. Then he finally turned and left us there in the doorway.

"I don't like that guy," Ollie said through gritted teeth.

"We've always bumped heads whenever he came by the armory."

We backed into the office and Olliare released a heavy sigh as he flopped down at his desk.

"Are we going to talk about this?" I asked.

"You know I'm not going to let this go. That little captain is jealous I picked you and not him for the promotion, and he's going to try to run around spreading rumors."

"No, Ollie." I pushed papers away to bring the map on his desk into view. "We need to talk about the Sudanese ships." I was certain the shock on his face was not only because of the surprising news, but also because I took no interest in the drama with the captain. I'm on Olliare's team, I'm allowed to be in his office, and his door is allowed to be closed because this is a private matter. Whatever rumors Luther wanted to spread didn't matter to me.

"You're not upset they don't want you there?"

"Do you even want to be there? Everyone prefers to just get orders and follow them in this kind of situation, instead of being part of the decision making."

He shrugged, and though I was flattered, the outcome of this meeting was far more important than my presence there.

"Alright," he grunted, "what do you have, Banks?"

"Looking at the map, the initial information we had was that Russia left what was once the Ukraine, by ship and were wading in the Mediterranean Sea. But there are also Russian ships that left Syria two days ago and they too are sitting in the Mediterranean Sea. Why they're just sitting there is the question we've been trying to answer."

"And we said they're preparing for an invasion on Israel, just getting all their ships in place."

"But why get ships on the sea when they can walk to Israel?"

"You really think Turkey and everyone else is just going to let Russia tromp through their country?"

"No but Syria might," I said, tapping the country on the map, "they've been linked to China *and* Russia in the past."

"Say what you mean, Banks," Ollie urged.

"I'm saying there's a possibility the ships are a decoy or are just supplies. Russian soldiers could be marching from Mother Russia as we speak. Cut through the smaller countries and walk the Turkish border to Syria."

"That's a lot and a very long trip. Why wouldn't they just invade with the ships?"

"Because they lose the element of surprise."

He squinted like it made sense, but it wasn't believable. Even for me, the idea was a little farfetched, but we needed to look at this from every angle.

"Okay." Ollie swept his hands over the map. "Let's say Russia is walking, and Turkey's alright with that and they're alright with their ships wading in the sea pointed at their land. What do we make of the *Sudanese* ships?"

"The Gulf of Aqaba is linked right to Israel which means Sudan is clearly part of this invasion. The only question, again, is why?"

Ollie rubbed his chin. "Well, we still can only speculate why Russia's invading and that was for resources. Israel is doing really well over there. America's just too prideful to ask for help. They'd give it if we asked, but," he shrugged, "I think this is our way of trying to get our feet back under us with all the debts and favors we owe."

"The famine blew our skirt up, exposed all our privacy, and just how weak we really are."

"Weakness..." Ollie reached for the papers of the writeup he had one of the lower ranks on our team put together. I watched him read quickly and mumble things to himself.

"What if Russia is trying to get us to use resources we don't have to weaken us even further?"

"You think they want to weaken us? But why?"

"Because we imposed the harshest sanctions on them. If we're too weak, we'll lift those sanctions."

"After all these years?"

"I don't know." He tossed his hands up in frustration. "I don't know anything anymore."

I walked around the desk and stood behind his chair, sinking my hands onto his firm shoulders. They were tight and full of stress as I began to massage him.

"Mmm," he murmured quietly. "I've always loved it when you did that."

"You've always loved when I touched you regardless."

He chuckled, shoulders bouncing in my grasp. "Major Banks, you do have a way to weaken me."

"I think I'm going to retire for the day."

"And go back to Johnson, after our time together?"

I pinched his shoulder.

He yelped.

I said, "*Jensen* shouldn't be left out in the dark when I'm not even needed now."

"*I* need you." Ollie turned in his leather chair.

With his sour gaze focused on me, I leaned forward and kissed his forehead. "I'll come back, Claudius."

He raised a brow. "First name? You must mean it."

"I do." I grabbed his hand. "I'll come back."

"This time, come back without all the baggage."

"What did you expect after a year?" I said as I moved to collect my things from the couch. "I moved on because I thought that was it."

"You didn't move on." Ollie met me at the door. "You just put a weak bandage over our memories together. But you never actually moved on."

"I guess you'll never know," I teased. "Maybe I'm planning to never return."

He leaned forward and kissed me. "You'll come back. We always come back to each other."

5

The North with All His Hordes

Zion

Dad left Monday. After the phone call I had with some government officials, I nearly walked out on stage just like Tony had suggested. The five years of peace had officially come to an end with the invasion of Taiwan. Russia's movement was briefly mentioned on the news, the focus was mostly on China's invasion. The world blamed China for ruining the peace we'd sustained for this long. It was like, if we blamed someone, then maybe that would make things sting a lot less. But nothing could make this any less of a problem than it actually was. And Russia's movement shouldn't be ignored.

I'd been staying with Mom since Dad left a few days ago. He wouldn't be home by Sunday, so we'd been busy making arrangements for a guest speaker to come in. I scrolled through the names of pastors on the computer. One of them was a woman I'd been with on a young leaders' retreat. I definitely couldn't call her.

I hated myself for corrupting every woman I came into contact with. I was not worthy of the position I held in church, but I was too embarrassed to give it up. I didn't want my secrets laid out in front of everyone, so I tried to deal with it on my own as best as I could. But these times seemed desperate and all I've been wanting to do is give Jala, Erica, Jennifer, anyone, a call.

I leaned back in the chair, the leather crinkled with my movement. I was sitting in my father's office at his long, wide desk. The room was a warm ivory color with brown wooden fixtures, and his walls were lined with large pictures of our family and his awards. It was a large office, a large role, one I was somehow expected to fill in my lifetime.

Truthfully, I didn't want to. It seemed hard, and I wasn't sure if I'd ever get tired of living life the way I liked. Rather, I didn't know if I'd ever find someone to settle down with. Maybe Jala, she had potential.

My father was the perfect example of a man. He loved God and then my mother. He put no one except the Lord above her and romanced her as often as he could. He was a pastor of a mega church, one that was seemingly perfect. There was only one bad apple—his son.

Me.

I was the corruption in the church, but he didn't know it. I had a good earthly example of what it meant to be a man, and a Heavenly Father who would help me. Yet, I always chose to oppose both of them, and I couldn't figure out why.

Maybe it was because God is perfect, and my father was on the heels of Abraham with his righteousness. I wanted to be righteous. That was what was most frustrating. I didn't have the discipline to be righteous, or a real relationship with God.

Sighing away my troubles, I focused back on the screen in front of me. I copied the list of names with the exception of a few I just couldn't face and sent them over to our secretary to contact.

"My work here is done," I said as I began closing the tabs on my computer.

There was one left open; a news tab. I'd been searching for updates on China, wanting to see if there'd be coverage of Dad with the president. But there hadn't been, so I figured it all must be private to protect my father. Our megachurch went beyond the borders of Missouri with many branches as far south as Louisiana, and as far north and eastern as Maine. There was also a west coast branch that was almost as big as our church here.

Even so, the popularity of The City on a Hill and my father only went so far. People were not too keen on religious entities influencing politics, specifically, the Christian religion.

With the downfall of Christianity in America, people stopped believing until the famine came along. That's when my father's ministry boomed alongside Missouri's importance. Missouri was just a mid-to-southern state once upon a time. The five years of peace changed that.

Missouri, known for its soybeans and corn, and plentiful irrigation via the drip system despite the droughts, *and* its extensive growing season, became an American pillar during the famine. It was one of the only states that was able to produce food after starvation put farms out of farmers, and disastrous heat had already ruined many other farmlands. Missouri held out, and eventually, because of the hungry thieves in the land, a military HQ moved to the state.

It was just the National Guard at first. But there'd been a fear that the US would be invaded if we didn't start paying off our debts, so half of Washington DC moved to Missouri. Plus, each branch of the US Military had a setup, and a joint headquarters was structured in the state.

Missouri was no longer just a little southern state. It was farming land protected by military forces and it housed important government officials. The best thing about that movement was that it was only known within the US that the officials had been split. Of course, the president, and very high-ranking officials stayed in Washington to keep the world from knowing since everyone knows where our president lives. But they managed to make some moves in the governing body, bringing folks down to us in case of an invasion.

I refreshed the news tab and saw the new headline:

China Threatens to Capture US Soldiers in Taiwan If They Do Not Retreat.

We'd just been threatened. The US had never taken lightly to threats. It was the same reason we sent the Speaker of the House, ages ago, to Taiwan when the whispers of a Taiwanese invasion first began.

China had threatened the US for deciding to stand with Taiwan back then. Now was no different. Though tensions had died down after a while and China and the US were on relatively good terms, I wasn't sure if tensions would die down again anytime soon. China had actually invaded Taiwan, and now the US had soldiers over there. Technically, we were at war.

I gathered my things from the desk and left the office to find my mother in our mansion. She had it custom built with heated floors and wide halls. The spindling in the pink and white marble walls made the entire mansion look like a photograph. The pillars with sculptures and vases lining the walls. Framed pictures of Black people, and German people frowned or smiled at you on your way through the house—a reflection of my family from my Black mother and German father. It was always so clean and pristine in this house, like no one lived here. The sparkling floors, and open floor plan made the house look even bigger, if that was even possible.

"Mom?" I called as I rounded the corner to one of the living rooms. She was sitting on a rustic orange couch, sipping grapefruit juice, and eating wheat toast.

"Mom—"

"Shh!" She threw a hand over her shoulder without even looking back at me. Snatching the remote, she mashed the volume a few levels before clutching her toast and glass.

She was watching After Dark, the infamous post-news show that made headlines nearly every airing (which was every day) because of their opinions and arguments. There were two news casters speaking. A woman dressed in a red dress with flat dark hair. And a man with a pudgy belly and balding head who leaned across the table, stressing a point.

"America has officially been threatened by the Chinese," the man was saying. "And we're still going to help? Take our boys out of there and get home to tend to our own problems!"

"Well, Matt," the woman started with a shrug, "we've really got to look at everything. The US is actually being backed into a corner with China's threat, and the hanging threat over Israel."

Matt threw his hand. "Chelsea, please. Israel? We've got bigger problems than Russian forces and Sudanese ships making regular routes. I don't know who's starting the foolishness that they're planning to invade Israel, but let's stop." He turned to the camera, thick white skin bunched into a grimace. "You guys don't have all the information so stop spreading things around. This is a very dangerous time. Rumors can get people killed!"

"I just don't understand how you can think it's a rumor, and why we shouldn't help Israel."

"I never said we shouldn't help Israel."

"That's what you insinuated. And you're convinced, for whatever reason, that Russian forces moving is just a routine? After four or five days, no movement on the waters? And Russia's been hidden the last *five* years? Come on, Matt, there's no way this isn't an attack or an invasion."

Matt rolled his eyes. "If we look at this realistically—"

"Well then let's just acknowledge that Israel is in danger if we're being realistic."

"Fine, Israel is being surrounded, and it is strange that Russia is moving after five years of silence, but—"

Chelsea cut in again, tossing her hair over her shoulder. "There is no *but*. Russia is moving in because they're fresh out of supplies after being locked behind that wall for five years. And now we're going to forsake our oldest ally?"

"Israel can stand on its own. We shouldn't even be helping *Taiwan*!"

The arguing continued, but suddenly their mouths were moving with no sound. My mother had muted the television as she sat in silence.

"Mom, what's wrong?" I knew something was up. That broadcast shed light on something that made the stillness in the room stifling.

"Do you know what the Gog Magog War is?"

"I know of it." I shrugged. "I never really studied it."

"Do you know why Russia is sitting on ships? Why Sudan is suddenly moving north?"

I stayed silent as she finally moved from the couch. Small bare feet met the carpet as she turned to face me. "Russia's

51

movement was an alert. Russia sitting on the Mediterranean Sea is a battle cry. They're signaling their allies that it's time to move. The only reason they haven't invaded yet is because they're waiting for other countries to get into place."

"What do you mean *other* countries? And where is all this coming from? No one is aligned with Russia. They couldn't be if they wanted resources during the famine."

"Russia sat in Ukraine behind a wall. You really think all five years they were just *sitting* there?" She tsked me. "Look at China. There's no way they sat around for five years being nice to the world just to be polite. They were making deals, plotting, and making plans for this invasion." She snorted as she set her grapefruit juice down on the glass coffee table in the center of the room.

"Taiwan isn't even the target," she said under her breath as she gazed at the floor for a moment. When she looked up, her hair fell from her face, and her icy glare made me shiver. "Your father didn't go see the president because they're friends. Nor has the president suddenly found salvation. Your father's sole reason for going was to convince the president to choose Israel and not Taiwan."

I shook my head as I came over to her. "Mom, I don't understand."

"The US is being forced to pick a side, Zion." She sounded annoyed with me now. "Russia and China have been working together for the past five years—whether we acknowledge it or not. But that leaked drone footage didn't lie. The only reason we didn't flag China for having dealings with a traitor is because, number one, China has no real allegiance to anyone. They've been self-sufficient for decades without telling anyone. And secondly—"

"We needed their help during the famine," I added.

She nodded, her bob flowing with the movement. I sat on the couch as my mother stood in the middle of the living room with her arms folded. She looked focused, angry even, as she thought deeply about what everything meant. I knew all this was serious, but with my mother getting involved now, I felt like it was the end of the world or something.

"We need to start preparing for the end."

Seriously?

"Whenever the Gog Magog war begins, that event will be the trigger for the rapture. Any moment after that is a free for all."

"Hold on," I stopped her. "Mom, I don't get any of this. Why is the world suddenly ending because of a war?"

"The Ezekiel thirty-eight war is when Russia and many other countries invade Israel. As Believers, we think this event is the last piece of the puzzle that has to fall into place before the rapture. What's happening right now is exactly what Ezekiel prophesied."

"If Israel's being invaded, why do *we* need to get prepared?"

"Because the moment America forsakes Israel is the moment she will fall. And after that, the rest of the world will follow suit."

6

When They Dwell Securely

Keoni

The door unlocked and I knew I was home alone. Jensen always left the garage door open for me when he was home. I was grateful he wasn't. His absence made this conversation a lot easier. I had time to think things through. Go over what I'd say.

I could leave without a goodbye, but I'm a soldier, not a coward. It was best that I faced him, told him straight out exactly what's been on my mind… though I'm not even sure how to put it into words.

Ollie came back into my life like a storm. When I opened the door to headquarters a few days back, I didn't think I was opening the door to my heart. I had strict rules to stay professional, but I broke promises to myself more than anyone else.

Like how I promised I wouldn't love again but ended up with Jensen. To be fair, in some way I had kept that promise. I didn't love Jensen, and it wasn't his fault. Our year together has been incredible, but as I sat in the office with Ollie for just four days, an entire year with Jensen had been forgotten. How could it be that four days overshadowed a year? The only answer was that I am in love, just not with Jensen.

Loving St. Olliare was dangerous. Though these four days have been filled to the brim with passion, they've also been filled with lust. And that lust turned heads. It caused eyebrows to raise and tongues to wag, spreading whispers.

If Ollie and I had just worked a regular office job, then maybe I wouldn't feel worried. However, we're in the military, where insubordination was one of the worst reasons for discharge.

A major with her superior ... what a joke.

But somehow, for Ollie, the relationship between us was no joke at all. I could guarantee that Ollie wanted this more than me; he was just afraid that I'd choose Jensen over him. Security or secrecy. Love was always more exciting when it was star-crossed, right?

I took a long shower. I had only showered twice while at the office, and the small locker room for women wasn't exactly what I'd call an ideal place to bathe. Considering the showers there had no doors, just a carved place in the wall where water spurted out at you. I was just thankful there was a bathroom at all.

All I'd need was two bags and my duffle bag of weapons I always kept under the bed. Jensen didn't know about that bag, so I'd put it in my truck before returning to finish packing my other bags when the front door opened. I waited for him in the room, continuing to pack as I listened to him move around the house in silence. I could remember when we first moved in together six months ago.

My mother, being the Bible believing woman she is, explained to me that shacking up with my boyfriend was wrong and I should wait until marriage. Thank God she knew nothing about Ollie or I'm sure I'd been killed by my own mama. But, at the time when she so indelicately explained the wrongs of shacking, I didn't care very much. However, as Jensen approached the bedroom, I realized something; one reason why marriage was better than moving in with someone, was because marriage was meant for life.

There is never an intention to move out when you're married. But shacking up meant there was nothing cleaving you to that person, and though freedom sat on the table, it was hard to say goodbye and face the mess you were about to create when everything was said and done.

Do I wish I'd married Jensen? No. But right then I wished I hadn't moved in with him. Then I could say goodbye and be done with this. I wouldn't have to endure the pain of packing my bags, sorting the pots and pans, and reliving the memories of our home until I found a new one. A better one.

"Whoa, Keoni?" Jenny's voice pulled me from my thoughts. "I didn't know you were home. Why didn't you tell me?" He dropped his bag at the bedroom entrance and rushed over to me. I was in his arms before I could speak. In my ear he whispered, "I missed you so much."

Frozen, I stood there for a second. All the times Jensen has held me, nothing has compared to this one. His lanky arms and tall figure squeezed me, and I found myself hugging him back. If he had been the sea, then I was a boat surrounded by his waters as he tugged me along to shore.

"I missed you too, Jenny." I just hadn't realized it until then. Jensen and I had only spent a few days apart, but so much had happened, it felt like a lifetime ago since the last time I saw him.

When he stepped back, there was a wetness on his face... he was crying. Someone missed me more than their heart could bear. How could I leave him? Jensen was exactly what I needed. Security and stability. However, Ollie was what I *wanted*. Scandalous and sensuous. Words with an 's' were indistinguishable sometimes.

"Jenny..." I chuckled as I used my sleeve to wipe at his tears, "don't cry."

He laughed too, cheeks turning red as he moved his head to follow my sleeve. "I really missed you, Ki. I dropped your uniforms off like you asked but they told me you were in a meeting."

"Yeah, we've had so many of those, I couldn't take it any longer. Thankfully, I wasn't needed today, so I came home. Thought we could spend the day together before returning back to headquarters tomorrow."

"Tomorrow? So soon?"

"Have you seen the news?" I asked as I moved from his embrace for the remote, but he stopped me.

"Wait," he said. His eyes shimmied over me as he pulled me back against him. His wide hands grazed down my back, tracing the curves of my body before he whispered, "I want this to last a little longer. They'll have you as much as they need you, and I know that's your job, but I need you too, Keoni."

Jensen was never so forward. He was gentle, and sometimes shy. Perfect for my brash personality at times. I wasn't used to this, not from him. And maybe that has always been the difference between Jensen and Ollie. Claudius has always been forward. He's been straight about what he wanted and honest about his feelings. Jensen was also honest, but in a roundabout way.

I usually had to pry things out of him; his feelings, his opinions, compliments. Jensen and I were good partners, excellent and fun partners even. Living together was easy for us, however, the romance and affection were very low between us.

But today, things were different.

"I-I'm sorry, Jensen," I said slowly.

When my eyes traced to his, I found that my initial apology would never reach him. His heart was already fragile, breaking it further by telling him I was leaving him was impossible. My own heart was breaking just looking at him.

"I didn't mean to be away for so long with such little contact," I said pathetically.

"It's okay." He shrugged. "You're here now, and that's all that matters to me."

When his lips met mine, a bout of guilt washed over me. But Jensen chased it away with his affection.

Since I ended up staying the entire weekend with Jensen, I came in early today. I figured Ollie would be there and would want an explanation before the day started. Trucking through the empty building, I found the stairs leading to Ollie's office. And I was right, he was there. The light reached from beneath his closed door, calling my attention. With a sigh, I braced myself for his reaction and opened the door without knocking.

"I was heartbroken. I thought you wouldn't return," he said in his voice that always seemed to hold a chuckle at the end of each sentence.

"It was the weekend, Ollie." I sighed. "I wasn't needed—"

"*Olliare*," he corrected.

I paused, glancing over at him for the first time since I entered his office. He was sitting at his desk, folders in front of him, and his face was void of all emotion—despite the teasing I *thought* I'd heard in his earlier tone.

"Are you seriously upset? If you needed me, all you had to do was call."

"Major Banks," he said as he stood from the desk. My eyes followed him around the room as he closed the distance between us and stood in front of me. "I've had an office set up

60

for you in case you decided to return to work. Thankfully, you have, so my team doesn't look like I picked a bunch of slack jobs. You'll have full use of—"

"Cut the crap, Ollie, seriously?"

I tossed my bags onto his couch as he corrected me once more. His voice flat. His face stony. "Olliare."

"What is wrong with you?"

He raised an eyebrow as he stepped closer to me, swallowing the last few inches of space between us. "Are you questioning your superior?"

"Yes, Ollie—"

"*Olliare!*" he sneered.

But I retorted incredulously, "*Claudius!*"

His face pinched in anger. I could see the pain washing over him. Staying with Jensen had truly hurt Ollie, but that was no excuse for his behavior now.

"How dare you?" I snapped through clenched teeth. "How dare you pull rank on me when I was the one trying to keep it professional? We spent a year apart, Olliare! We both moved on with our lives, like we were supposed to! What am I supposed to tell Jensen after a year? That I'm leaving him for my old fling after a couple days' reunion!? It's not that easy. Commitment is a real thing, though I know it's never meant much to you."

"What are you talking about?"

"You always get mad and push me away. You get over our arguments with the help of other women. You get over your boredom with *fun* dates. Not once have I ever done that to you.

61

I waited for you every time to come back to me. And now you're angry because—after a year and some change—I moved on like we said we would?"

"Some of us couldn't just move on."

I frowned. "You think it was so easy to up and leave? I was eighteen when I met you. Young and naïve. I had never even had sex before."

He flinched, his eyes racing over me like he couldn't believe it. I'd never told Ollie that I was a virgin when we'd met. I'd always been athletic, so the proof was missing after our first time, but the soreness was still there for me.

I snatched my bags from his couch and rushed for the door when he reached out and grabbed my arm.

I whirled around and shoved him. "Get off me! You don't get to pull rank when you're punishing me for something that has nothing to do with work!"

"It has everything to do with work!" he yelled back. "Keoni, you wouldn't be here if it wasn't for me. You're here *with* me, *because* of me." He slammed his hands against his chest. "I've done everything I could to show you that I care, and you turn around and reject me for some scumbag?"

"I have never rejected you," I seethed. My anger was reaching a boiling point and I took a deep breath to still myself. Tears were burning like fire in my eyes, but I wouldn't let them fall. "When have I ever not waited for you to return? We have always said we'd come back to each other, but you know better." I jabbed a finger at him, poking his broad chest. "You know I have never been the one to walk away. I have always been the one waiting! So I'm sorry for thinking that you would have more faith in me and believe that I wouldn't just abandon you."

With a huff, I turned on my heels, heading for the door when his voice came weakly behind me. "Wait, Keoni. I'm sorry. I'm just frustrated—"

"Yeah? And what about me? How do you think it makes me feel returning home, lying through my teeth, just to return here for you to treat me like *this*?"

I shook my head as I grabbed the door and opened it. When I glanced back over my shoulder, I found Ollie standing there with a pleading look on his face, but the damage was done.

When I returned home, I hadn't expected to enjoy my time with Jensen. In fact, I was thinking only of Ollie. But Jensen's sadness broke my heart, and I couldn't leave. Yet, I still wanted to return to Ollie. I never stopped thinking about him the entire weekend. Had even caught myself daydreaming about him when Jensen was showering or out of the room.

The next day, I returned to work with every intention of not returning to Jensen later, or at least weaning away from him over time. My plan was to let the distance drive him down the road, ways away from me.

Huffing air between my lips, I stepped out the door at HQ and did an about-face, saluting my superior. Ollie didn't raise his hand; he didn't salute me back. He looked distraught, angry, and tired. But not at me, just at himself. I had played my part in creating this mess, however, Ollie was not guiltless either. I didn't wait for him to salute me or give me a command.

Dropping my hand, I swallowed my tears. "Thank you for seeing me so early, and for the office, General Saint-Olliare."

7

I Will Fall Upon the Quiet People

Zion

"We're heading into week three with no one, Mom. Pastors are in demand, being called to preach all over about the End Times." I watched my mother closely as she sat across from me. We were in my father's office, trying to book another guest speaker in Dad's absence.

The thing about the Christian community is… the church is quick to jump onto a prophecy. From the famine to the invasion of Taiwan, to the threats against the US, churches have been begging End Times prophets and teachers to hold classes, preach sermons, and break down the Book of Revelation. Finding someone to fill Dad's shoes has not been an easy task.

A City on A Hill hadn't begun any prophetic teaching. Mom said God told her it wasn't time yet. People still needed to be preached to, they still needed to hear the Truth—to learn about other things besides famine and pestilence.

"People are preaching that we've got to get right because the End is here. But everyone's stopped preaching on *how* to get right," Mom had said.

Salvation was still at hand. Prophecies would unfold, and the truth would be revealed. There was no reason to rush into teaching about the unfolding events, at least not at our church. God had a different plan for my mother. We had been spending our free time stocking the church's bunker, and the storage rooms. Mom said we needed to be physically *and* spiritually prepared for the End. That meant resources would be scarce, medicine would be short, but faith would need to be high.

"Well, I can continue leading the prayer meetings at five in morning. You'll do Sunday service and Bible Study. You think you're ready?" Mom asked.

"No," I answered almost too quickly.

Mom looked up from the little calendar she was writing in. Her glasses slipped down her nose and she peered over the rims at me. "Why are you answering like that?"

I took a quick breath. "Sorry, Mom. I just don't think I can be ready by Sunday. There's a lot of preparation to go into a sermon."

She smiled, though she looked relieved as she reached for my hands. "Sweetheart, I know you may feel a little anxious but trust me, if you just let the Holy Spirit lead you, you'll be fine. You've been training for this all your life."

"I know but…" I squeezed her hands and dropped my head. "There's communion on Sunday. I can't lead that."

"Of course you can. During a time like this, when everything's going haywire, you need to break bread. The Body of Christ will make you whole, and the Blood of Jesus will wash away sins, sickness, and diseases. It'll protect you during chaos like this. You remember the death angel in Egypt?"

Sighing, I raised my head, and saw that my mother was as cheerful as one could be about their son's first sermon. I should've been happier, but knowing all that I'd done in secret was eating away at me. I may do many sinful things, but defiling God by standing in that pulpit wasn't one of the things I was willing to do.

Maybe if I told her the truth, she won't want me—

"Well, do you remember or not?"

"Huh? Remember what?"

She pouted. "The death angel in Egypt? Are you listening?"

"Yes, Mom, I remember and I'm listening."

She nodded. "The blood over the doorpost protected the Children of Israel from the death angel that passed by. It'll be the same thing for believers as the times get shaky. God will make a distinction for us because we'll be covered under the Blood of Jesus. Which means sickness, harm, you name it, will go right on by us. And you want to know a secret about the death angel?"

"I think you'll tell me anyway," I joked, though it was all sarcasm.

Mom laughed anyway and nodded.

"The secret about the death angel is this: death cannot conquer life. The life of the flesh is in the blood. That's Leviticus chapter seventeen and verse eleven. Since there was blood over the doorpost of the Hebrews, that meant there was life." Her smile stretched from ear to ear as she went on to explain more.

"Death could not conquer life because the blood on the door posts was indicative of Jesus' life protecting us. And Jesus conquered death, a life traded for our life. And the significance of this comes from the life of Christ. During His life, Jesus saved, delivered, healed, set free, multiplied, the list goes on." She waved a hand. "So, when we are covered in the Blood of Jesus, death cannot come for us because of the life of Christ. Bad situations cannot come because of the prosperous life of Jesus. We can be healed because of the Blood of Jesus. His life, His blood, is our power. Tell me what the source of that power is?"

"I… don't know."

She then asked, "What brought Adam to life?"

"The breath of God?"

"Exactly. Blood carries oxygen. The breath of God is the oxygen of the Blood of Jesus. God is the source of the power of the life of Christ, because His Spirit enabled Jesus to save, heal, deliver, all of that."

I sat for a second, amazed at my mother. She was a small woman who hardly said more than a simple 'God bless you' at church. But she was the most powerful person I knew. Even more than Dad.

"Why don't you teach that this Sunday?" I shrugged as I let her hands go to sit back in the chair. "Teach about the protection of the Blood of Jesus. I think people need to hear that."

"Maybe."

I frowned at her. "You know the church doesn't care about you being a woman, right? They just want to hear about Jesus." She'd preached before, and we'd had other lady Pastors preach as guests too. Heck, *anyone* would make a better preacher than me. There was so much sin in my life, I was sure God would strike me down if I stepped foot into the pulpit. But Mom seemed apprehensive.

She gave me a warm smile. "Son, this has nothing to do with my gender. The congregation needs to hear this message from their next leader."

"*You* can lead them, Mom."

"I know, but I truly prefer to rest in the background."

Groaning, I turned the chair away from her to look out the office window. "Fine," I finally said. Maybe this was my chance to actually set things right with God.

My phone vibrated, and I grabbed it off the desk to check it. There was a text from Jala.

Are you free tonight?

Yeah, we should talk.

Everything was suddenly coming together. I wasn't going to let my chance to make things right with God slip by me with the world about to spin off its axis.

"Mom, I've got to run home, but I'll be back by tomorrow."

"Home?" She nodded without looking up from her calendar. She'd gone back to organizing things on it. "You haven't been there in a while. You sure you want to go back?"

It felt like a warning, like maybe I shouldn't go back. I'd been staying with Mom since Dad had been busy flying in and out of town. I'd gotten used to life away from that environment. But I'd already told Jala I wanted to talk to her, and I needed to do this.

"Yeah, Mom." I stood and pushed my phone into my pocket. "Why wouldn't I?"

"Sometimes being alone is a bad environment itself—when you're left to your own thoughts of doubt."

Mom wasn't warning me about Jala at all. She was afraid I was going to go home and realize I didn't want to preach on Sunday. It was the total opposite. I wanted to go home to set things right with Jala, cut her off, and start making things right with God. I couldn't dishonor Him and mark myself for death by preaching when my hands were dirty right in His pulpit. Plus, leading communion. There was no way I could lead a Holy ceremony like that with an unclean temple. I had to get right.

70

"You don't have to worry. I'm going home to start preparing for Sunday. I just need to get a few things worked out first and then I'll be studying through the weekend."

She looked up at me with stars in her eyes. "I'm so proud of you. I can't wait to tell your father. I know he'll be proud too."

Coming around the desk, I leaned forward and kissed her head.

— ÷ —

I picked up all the mail that'd been shoved through the slot beneath the front door of my loft. The place was the same as I'd left it; neat, and dark. Ebony walls with floor-to-ceiling portraits of prominent figures in American history lined my walls. Nude carpeted floors made my steps soft as I moved from the hardwood floors of my foyer to my living room.

I tossed the mail onto the square quartz table and fell onto my couch with a sigh. "God, I'm really going to be different after today, aren't I? I won't do the things I've always done anymore. I'll finally be better… I'll be worth something to You." The last statement made me smile to myself. Being worth something to God was all I'd ever wanted deep down.

I wanted to be the man my parents thought I was, be the man I knew God made me to be. But the fight with the flesh was really a war. A civil war that has left me ruined by guilt and shame. Today, though, I would be able to declare victory. I'd be able to declare that God was the reigning champion, and my heart had been given back to Him.

When the doorbell rang, I almost jumped for joy. I sprang off the couch and onto my feet in an instant.

"One second!" I raced to the door and snatched it open.

Then I blinked. And stared.

"Abigail?" my voice cracked.

"Hi, Zion," she said flatly. Big almond eyes that I'd adored for nearly a year, blinked away from me and into my apartment. "Are you alone?"

"Yeah, but now's not a good time, Abbey."

She wiped her nose and glanced around like she was nervous or watching out for someone. I had always been careful not to let women hang around the door, but Abigail, just like every other girl, never seemed to mind or care. They knew we couldn't be seen together at the times they'd come and leave my place, so they made quick work to be in and out.

"Listen, Abbey—"

"I promise, it'll just take a second," she cut me off.

"I can't." I shrugged. "I'm trying to get my life together and I don't need any distractions. I'm sorry, Abbey, but I have to go." I backed into my apartment to pull the door shut when she slammed a palm against it.

"Wait, a second," she pled.

"Cut it out," I snapped quickly as I ripped the door back open.

She tripped forward, straightening herself; that's when I noticed her baggy clothes. Abigail was never one to dress

72

'down.' She always wore flashy clothes that caught my eye, splits in her skirt that were just a little too high, nothing to yap about. Shirts that were cut just the slightest bit too low.

Abbey was a secretive woman with ways of seduction that forced Jala to do everything she could to keep my attention on her. But that wasn't hard once Abigail stopped coming to church three months ago. I never got the chance to check in since Jala was always taking up all my time.

"What is it?" I asked hotly. "Do you need money or something?" I dug furiously into my pocket but stopped when I heard the elevator ding. My head flew up in an instant, and the anger on Abbey's face melted into confusion as she stared back at me.

She must've picked up on the horror I was feeling with having two women I'd been sleeping with at my place at the same time.

Jala and Abbey had bad blood because Abbey found out about Jala when I'd promised her there was no one else. Jala's just always been eager to scrap, so it was suffocating when the two came to the same service instead of Abbey coming to second service one Sunday morning. I was actually relieved when she stopped coming altogether, especially after the two got into a screaming match in the parking lot.

I, of course, ended up breaking them apart. That was the last time Abbey and I had been physically involved. But it was also one of the wildest nights in my entire life. Because when Abbey left my place for work, Jala came by until morning.

I told you; I've never been a great guy. But this is the part where I get my act together. I promise.

"Abbey, just come inside." I reached for her hand, but the action halted when Abbey's name was called down the hall.

She looked down to find Jala who was once prancing down the hall, now thundering towards us.

"You're still seeing her?" Abbey asked softly as she looked back at me. The hall was long, so we had a moment to exchange words, but I could barely speak. I was taken aback by her stillness. There was no aggression or aggravation, Abigail seemed thoroughly shocked, but there was something else on the brim of her levelheadedness.

"It's not what you think," I finally managed as Jala stepped in front of Abigail and snapped, "What is this, Zion? I'm not here the moment you ask, and you get *her* to come over?"

"No, Jala—baby—listen. It's not like that at all."

"Then what is it?!"

"Can you keep your voice down?" I seethed.

"Piss off, Zion. You should've thought about that before you started cheating on me."

Abigail finally moved from behind Jala and scowled. "You've got a serious problem if you think you deserve to be treated with dignity or respect. You started sleeping with Zion when I was with him *first*, and you knew it."

Jala looked her up and then down, and then back up once more before cackling over her shoulder.

"*Hey*," I snapped, grabbing her arm, "cut it out."

"Or what?" she jerked away so hard, I almost stumbled.

74

"Or I'm going to tell my father that we've been sleeping together. He'll sit me down, but he'll remove your father from the Church Board and make him get a job outside of the church."

Jala's face was cramped with anger, like any more frustration and her pretty little face would crack. She whirled away, exhaling loudly, and bumping Abigail as she walked by.

"We still need to talk," I called after her.

Stopping abruptly, Jala turned to me and said coldly, "Don't ever speak to me again."

I watched her a moment, hips rocking with every step she took. I thought it'd be hard to see Jala go, but now it was like watching a stick of dynamite get thrown away before blowing everything up.

"Was she why we couldn't talk?"

I looked back at Abbey and sighed. She wasn't going to let this go, so I let her inside.

Glancing around as she stepped inside, she said, "The place hasn't changed."

"You're acting like you haven't seen it in ten years. We stopped seeing each other three months ago." I walked into the kitchen and grabbed some iced tea from the fridge. "I've got tea. I know you liked it."

She laughed as she rounded the corner still fully dressed. She was wearing a big fur jacket, with a baggy sweatshirt underneath and baggy sweatpants that bunched at the top of her boots. "I still love iced tea."

"You want a glass?"

"Sure." She nodded.

My eyes lingered on her a little longer. There was something off about Abigail, but something so right about her at the same time.

"Is everything alright?"

She didn't speak as I poured her a glass of tea. When I passed it to her, our hands touched and she flinched, dropping the glass. It shattered, spilling brown liquid all over my freshly polished hardwood floors.

"I'm sorry," she said shakily. "I'm so clumsy, I just keep—"

"Abbey," I called over her prattling. She stopped, but never raised her eyes to mine. "Forget the tea." I stepped over the glass and stood in front of her. "What is going on with you?"

"Zion..." Milky brown skin and baby doll curls were all over her shoulders. "Zion, there's something I need to tell you."

"What is it?"

She reached for me, and I caught her hand. Abigail had always been the most sensitive woman I'd ever been with. She came from a small town in Minnesota before she moved here to Missouri. She was a sheltered girl and was here for college. She'd been in her third year when we met. A friend of hers had told her to try coming to church and she did, but I ruined that for her. I'd ruined what real Christianity looked like.

"Zion, I'm pregnant."

I let her hand go and stepped back. "What?"

"*Please*, I'm sorry, Zion."

"You told me you were on birth control."

"There was something wrong with my intrauterine device. It wasn't releasing the hormones right, but I didn't know it."

"You didn't know it," I repeated darkly.

She shook her head. "Zion, I swear. I would never do this to you. I'm—"

"Shut up!" I hollered. "Shut up!"

Abbey was crying in the corner of my kitchen, whimpering apologies through her tears. I was livid. My mouth went dry, and there was a raging heat that made me break out into a sweat. I wanted to believe that Abbey really didn't know about her intra-whatever, but I was so angry.

Angry at myself for being an idiot. Angry that I couldn't make this all just go away. I may have threatened Jala, but I didn't mean a word I'd said. I was only turning to God now because my sins had been a secret. But what if they're not secret anymore? What am I supposed to do?

"Are you sure it's mine?" I asked, turning to face Abbey.

She glared at me. Insulted. "Yes. I wasn't with anyone else but you."

"How am I supposed to believe that?" I tossed my hands up. "This could be some sick revenge plot because you're mad that Jala and I started fooling around when we were still together."

She straightened and lifted her chin, though tears still streaked her face. "What you did with Jala hurt me, but I would

77

never do this to you!" She screamed the last part of her sentence, yelling for the first time ever.

Outside of the bedroom, Abigail was very mild tempered. She'd always been an incredibly quiet and shy girl. The sort of submissive woman church folk liked to brag about. The sort of woman who obeyed without question. The sort of woman who was easily abused by men like me.

I had used Abbey. I had stolen her innocence and then broken her heart, and now she was back with more mess to dump on me. Mess that I'd created. Seeing her holler like this made me fall silent.

"You cheated on me!" she screamed. "I was always loyal to you, Zion. But I was never enough for you. No one has ever been enough for you. That's why you can't stop. Because you don't love anyone but yourself!" She wiped at her tears before turning to leave. "This was a mistake."

"Abigail, wait."

"For what? For you to accuse me of cheating on you again?"

"No." I walked over to her, and she shied away from me as I leaned over. "What are you going to do with it?"

"*It?*" She glanced around like she was looking for help. "*It* is a *baby*! A human life! We can't just get rid of a baby!"

"Yes, we can," I said flatly.

Her eyes were as wide as the moon.

"You're kidding me, right?" she whispered.

"No, I'm not. I want you to get rid of it."

"I'm not killing my child." She shook her head.

78

"I said get rid of it!" My voice came out a snarl, shocking both of us, but Abigail didn't back down.

"You don't get to tell me what to do!" she yelled fearlessly.

"Abigail, this isn't about you!"

"Oh my goodness." She let out a single chuckle. "You're seriously worried about your own reputation instead of our child—"

"Don't call it my child."

"I'm not sticking around for this."

She turned to leave, but I pushed by her and raced to the door and double locked it.

"What are you doing?"

"You're not leaving until we're getting in a car and driving to the closest clinic."

"Missouri doesn't even allow abortions!"

"Then get comfy until I get free time to go to Illinois!"

"You *murderer!*" She rammed her hands into my chest, shoving me hard against the door. She was beating my chest, pounding it, and screaming at me. Slowly, I wrapped my arms around Abbey, and her frantic crying turned into a somber song against me.

I was scared. I was angry. I didn't know what to do but only because Abbey was right. My only concern was making things right for me, which meant I didn't have room for something like a baby. Babies were permanent stains, constant reminders of all the wrong you've done. I didn't know if I could take that.

What would my parents think? The congregation? What did God think?

8

My Wrath Will Be Roused in My Anger

Zion

Abigail is pregnant. Her belly has a bump, and her belly button is beginning to protrude a little. After her hysterical crying, she removed her jacket and baggy clothes. She said she'd been hiding it the best she could, but she was growing more every day now. Though she was only in her second trimester, Abbey was normally a small woman, and the pregnancy weight was showing right along with the bump.

I ended up agreeing to let her stay in my guest suite, but that didn't mean we were suddenly together again. In fact, Abigail and I haven't said much else to each other in the last three days since she first showed up. I've been keeping myself busy at church, away from her and the growing baby.

If I'm honest, I really didn't want a child. But I knew an abortion was wrong, despite my initial response. I did, in the dark corners of my heart, still want an abortion. I wanted it gone. I'd rather just repent and deal with the aftermath later. It wasn't like I didn't have a hundred other sins to beg forgiveness for. What was one more?

At the same time, I couldn't fully commit to that idea because of my Christian upbringing. I'd done everything else wrong, so this should've been easy, but it just wasn't. An abortion felt *really* wrong, but that's what happens with a public sin.

When it was just me sneaking girls over, it was fine. Now the revelation of the result of all the sneaking around had begun to grow… literally. That meant the hidden sin was more dangerous than the public sin, as our Father who sees in secrets, rewards in secret or publicly, He also does the same with His judgment.

So, I'm caught between a rock and a hard place.

Abbey couldn't stay hidden forever, and she didn't want to. She mentioned when she first arrived that she was thinking of returning to church, but I told her she couldn't. Though no one else at church may suspect a thing between us if Abbey returned pregnant, *Jala* would know who got her pregnant. And I couldn't run the risk of her telling anyone.

Me getting Abbey pregnant would certainly overshadow anything that'd happened between Jala and me. If I was going to start over, I'd have to come clean with everything myself. Finding out from me was the best thing for the church and my parents, but did I really want to tack on an abortion to my list of sins?

"God?" I whispered in my bathroom. I was lying on the cold white floor, crying as quietly as I could. It had been a part of my routine since Abbey moved in. I had no idea what to do. No idea if she should be here despite there being no romance between us. Though my mother told me before I moved out, that living with someone you had history with or were interested in was not a good idea no matter how friendly or unfriendly we were. She said it opened the door for a temptation that most weren't strong enough to overcome. So I guess I had my answer to that, but I still had no idea about anything else.

"God, I don't want to put her out because she's pregnant. But I know it's wrong. Everything is all wrong. I was supposed to be starting over! All I've done is backslide. How can I ever prepare to preach on Sunday?" I wept softly against the floor as I lay there begging God for an answer.

After a while, I got up and cleaned myself up. The only thing I got out of prayer was my blatant disregard for my mother's warning. Opening the door to temptation was dangerous. I knew that all too well. But was it really alright to put her out? Should I really just get rid of her?

Maybe she should go home for now, and we could figure things out that way. But the thought of doing the right thing was washed away by a violent bout of worry and anxiety. Fear of the truth coming out, and I could feel the teeth of rebellion biting a little deeper.

"Abbey?" I called as I left the bathroom.

A few moments later she peeked her head out from the guest suite and I said, "I've got to go to my mother's house. There's food in the fridge."

"Your mother," she stepped out wearing a silk night gown trimmed in lace, with a matching white silk robe.

She looked good... really good.

"How is she?" Abigail asked.

"Who?" I blinked, coming back from my ridiculous pregnant Abbey fantasy.

She squinted. "Your mother? I haven't seen her in a while." As she waited for an answer, she crossed an arm over her chest and gently brushed a curl away from her face with her other hand. Abbey's timidness had always been one of her best qualities. She was melting all my fortitude from such a simple gesture.

"Oh, she's good," I nodded, glancing off. Maybe it was because she was carrying *my* child, or maybe because I hadn't seen Abbey in three months. But today, I was oddly attracted to her.

It's funny, my mother's warning was loud and clear, however, it was easy to ignore as I looked at the very radiant woman before me.

"Well," she said after a moment of silence ticked by, "you should probably go. I don't think you should keep her waiting."

"Yeah, I'd better go."

"Zion," she said quickly as I headed for the door.

I rested my hand on the smooth silver handle, and glanced back at her. The sun was casting its rays around her, giving her a backlight. Abbey had always been beautiful, but this pregnancy was making her irresistible, I think.

"We should talk when you get home. I think there are things we need to discuss."

"Like what?" I said, letting go of the handle.

"Like are we keeping the baby or not?"

I paused. "I-I-I thought you wanted it? Or the baby," I corrected myself quickly.

She took a shaky breath, her hands roving over the little bump. "I want this more than anything. I feel like this baby has already made me stronger and I don't even know the gender." She chuckled, but there was a tear rolling down her cheek. "Sorry," she whispered as she swiped the tear away.

"Abbey, listen. I don't know what we should do. I know an abortion is wrong, but I just don't have the time to spare for a child. And I'm not ready for that." I stepped forward and reached for her hand. She took it, and our fingers intertwined like they used to. "But I don't know if I can take this from you. I can't ask you to do this for me. I should've been a better Christian, a better leader. But I failed God, and you. The only thing I can do is make things right."

"You didn't fail me, Zion." She moved into my arms, and I held her tight. "I... I wanted to tell you right away, but I didn't know how."

"I should've been there for you."

She shook her head. "No, I needed that time to accept this. Accept that I'm about to be a mother." She paused to look up at me. Pouty pink lips begged with desperation for me to kiss them. I was going to until she started again. "If you won't ask me to get rid of the child, then I won't ask you to be part of the child's life. A life for a life. You spare the baby's and I'll spare yours. We'll stay away, and you'll never have to wonder about us. I'll never even ask for child support."

Her eyes were pleading with me too now. Except there wasn't a cry for lust in them, there was a hope that I'd accept the deal she'd offered. I would be free, and no one would ever have to know that I'd made a horrible mistake. But could I trust Abbey? Could I really let her walk away with my own child and never question it? Was this the right thing to do?

Of course it wasn't. At least not on a moral level.

"Abbey, I—" My phone blared and we jumped apart. "Sorry," I waved a hand, "it's my mother. I'm running late." I lowered my phone to see Abbey wearing a small smile, but the pleading was still in her eyes. "You don't have to run away. I'm going to take care of you and the baby. I just need to tell everyone first," I said. "So, just give me a little time, and I promise I'll make this right for you."

She looked stunned, like she'd been expecting the worst. I could've been offended, but after giving each other the silent treatment for three days because I told her to get an abortion, I completely understood her shock.

"I've got to go or my mother will kill me," I chuckled.

"Thank you," she whispered. "Thank you, Zion."

It really wasn't my choice. Abigail was going to keep that baby no matter what. She spent three days coming up with a plan to preserve the child, and she was becoming a mother already.

I pecked the top of her head and left her standing in shock in the middle of the foyer.

— ÷ —

When I arrived at the mansion, Dad's car was out front.

"Zion, where were you?" Mom didn't even greet me. She grabbed my hand and led me through the house until we rounded the corner where my father sat in the living room.

Initially, I was relieved by his presence. Now that my father was home, I didn't have to preach on Sunday. I could spend more time getting myself back on the right path with God and get Abbey out of my place. However, Abbey and the pressing pregnancy issue went out the window when my father looked up at me... he wasn't sad or angry, he was scared.

"Sit down, Zion."

I nodded, forgetting the greetings of relief I was going to give him. Beyond the fear, was exhaustion. My dad had spent three weeks in meetings with the president, giving him spiritual advice on decisions made on military and international relations. With all the drama going on in my personal life, I had forgotten the rest of the world was in chaos. People were afraid everywhere. Major countries were going to war. The US was under threat.

We had just gotten back on our feet from the famine, now everything was crumbling.

I shifted on the sofa as my father's tired voice filled the room. "There are things that haven't hit the news yet," he said solemnly. "But I'm going to tell you and your mother first. Rhoda told me that you guys organized some fallout shelters and filled up our pantries in the church. That was a good thing you two did."

"Dad, what's going on?" I asked anxiously.

"It's here, son, the end of the world."

I glanced at my mother who'd taken her place beside my father on the couch, she bobbed her head in agreement with my father's words.

"The end of the world? Like the rapture and stuff?"

"Yes," my father said unemotionally. "Israel is completely surrounded. We've gotten word from the birds that there are nations, Biblically in line with the prophetic words of Ezekiel, all on standby. Turkey, Iran, Libya and Egypt, Azerbaijan, to name a few." He was counting them out on his large thick fingers when my mother chimed in.

"These nations are making moves to invade Israel on every side, and they're not afraid. But Israel isn't either."

"Then why are you?" I questioned my father.

His brows lowered in sadness as he glanced away from me. "A draft notice is going out because the Secretary of Defense is settled on helping Taiwan and not letting China threaten us. The country needs soldiers, and no one's signing up."

"Your father has been assured by the president that you won't be drafted under the clergy pretense."

I exhaled, thankful for being a deacon though I had truly abused that privilege. Now I definitely had to do right by God.

Swallowing thickly, I asked, "So, you're afraid for the draft?"

My father shook his head in the silence. "I'm afraid because of the Secretary of Defense. He's a real brash guy, we bumped heads a few times while I was there. He really isn't religious at all, and he has a particular problem with the Christian faith."

"I see." I slid my eyes to my mother, and she offered an explanation to my father's patchy answer.

"The Secretary of Defense didn't like the president taking advance from your father. He didn't like him in the White House and gave Jillian all kinds of problems. He had a really hard time convincing President Warrick not to go all in for Taiwan like the Secretary of Defense had suggested."

"But why does going all in for Taiwan make you afraid?"

"If we're going all in for Taiwan," my father explained, "then we've got nothing left for Israel. And once America forsakes Israel, God will forsake *us*."

I slowly pulled a shoulder up, gaging my parents' startled reactions. "But the rapture is going to happen soon, *we'll* be fine, right? Like, us Believers." I was circling the room with my finger when neither of them spoke. The tense silence forced a nervous fidget from me as I adjusted in my seat. "Dad?" I said, "we'll be fine, *right?*"

"The rapture is on the horizon, but we don't know how long after the war begins, how long after America forsakes Israel, before it actually happens."

"Hold on," I shook my head, "I thought once the war began, we'd be raptured?"

"We can't say for certain, Zion. We may be here when God's protection leaves America."

I sat back in my seat and stared ahead. America had been on a decline for the last decade, *at least*. Mom told me that a war would begin if we turned our back on Israel. However, I never really expected the US to do that. I expected Dad to return home, and the rapture scare would be over. But that wasn't the case.

With a great sigh, my eyes finally reached my father and mother. I'm certain I looked as fearful and dreadful as my father when I first saw him.

"America is about to fall," I said slowly. "She's about to finally lose her status as the greatest and most powerful country in the world."

Neither of them disagreed.

9

Be A Guard for Them

Claudius

China issued a threat to the US weeks ago when they first began their invasion of Taiwan. They told us not to send in any soldiers or give any more aid to Taiwan or we'd be in danger of territorial immorality. Meaning simply, China truly believed Taiwan was theirs to reclaim, just like Nepal, Tibet, and parts of India.

They didn't think the US should be interfering with their personal problems with Taiwan. To them, Taiwan was an 'escapade.' They're a small child throwing a temper tantrum because their parent, China, told them they couldn't have their way. No parent wants someone else to discipline their child.

Major Banks and I agreed we couldn't completely disregard Taiwan, but we knew the presence of our soldiers were more offensive to China since they have our weapons.

91

Having a map and reading it the best way you can is totally different from the one who made the map telling you the best course of action. The US was the cartographer, in this scenario (as far as weapons went) so China didn't totally have the upper hand.

Banks and I also agreed not to send any more bodies into Taiwan, but we're just two people, and we were overruled ultimately by our counterparts and the Secretary of Defense. Keoni didn't know that yet. She also didn't know that we've got to prepare for China finding out about our soldiers being in Taiwan and fighting. Because whenever they do find out, we'll need enough soldiers to counter whatever attack they'll try to launch on our men. The Taiwanese battlefield was about to enlarge.

Keoni would know all this if she wasn't restricting me just to email communication. There are some things that can't be passed along in email, it's better to talk in person. But when I go to her office she's not there. And when I summon her to mine, she sends a liaison in her place with the excuse that she's swamped.

I haven't seen the woman in three weeks and four days. Yes... I am counting. I didn't mean it when I gave her an office. I was angry. She went, and undoubtedly, made love to her boyfriend, who's a complete idiot, and then came back and expected me to be alright with it? Maybe pulling rank was a little cold, or a lot cold, but if she would give me a chance to explain myself, she'd see I didn't mean any of it.

"St. Olliare," General Hunter called behind me. I turned and he jogged up to me and patted my shoulder. "How are you, Claudius?"

"I'm well, sir, how are you?"

"You're so formal these days. Everything alright?"

I snorted. "General, you're still my superior despite our love for golf."

The short three-star general laughed and patted my shoulder with a leathery hand. "You must seriously be having problems if you're calling me your superior. You don't respect anyone's rank."

"That's not true," I said as we turned a corner, keeping in step with each other. "I respect rank, but I'm the guy who handles everything for you higher-ups. I know your crap and I'm not buying it," I joked.

He was smiling and nodding along as we continued down the hall. "Just like Major Banks, she apparently isn't taking *your* crap."

I stopped on a dime, and he slowed to a stop and glanced back with a devious smile. "Don't tell me you thought that got by me? The rumors going around this place travel faster than a speeding bullet."

"What rumors?"

"Walk, and I'll tell you."

I took a deep breath to recompose myself and got moving beside him. Soldiers stepped in and out of rooms with paperwork, nodding their heads at us as we walked through the headquarters. Hunter and I were close, but Keoni was my little secret. I would never share anything about us or betray her trust, and possibly break her heart even more. Kiki and I have never been on easy street, but I wasn't about the rip up the black top and throw down pebbles and glass for us to drive over either.

"She's sexy," General Hunter said beside me.

I wasn't one to talk about a woman I was serious about with anyone, not even Hunter. But he knew that, and that's why he was poking me. If I didn't play this game with him, things would only get worse.

"She is *very* sexy," I smirked at him, "but Major Banks and I are just totally different."

"Really?"

"Yeah." I shrugged, though it wasn't a total lie. Keoni and I had different ways of showing affection. Keoni's affection was in her loyalty, her ability to love me no matter what. Mine was in providing for her. Putting my neck on the line for her every time I stated her opinion in meetings she didn't even attend.

I'd promoted her, or at least shuffled paperwork to make her name look better. And she was attractive, physically, and mentally. She had a lovely figure, and a stony personality that wasn't as cold as it seemed.

When she returned with a purple heart, Keoni had shut down. Before that, she was girly, and loving. But, after losing her vision in one eye and gaining a few scars, she became like ice. Eventually she warmed up to me again, and on the night of her ceremony, we sneaked out to a hotel afterward, but things took a while to get started between us.

I'll never forget the way she cried when I confessed to loving her that night. What a geeky thing to do, confess to a young girl you've been sleeping with, but it was true on some level back then. However, I don't think I really meant until it was too late. That year without Keoni had been the hardest year of my entire life.

"Well," Hunter's nasally voice caught my attention as we slowed to stop at his office. "I'm just saying, you two sharing an office is a little suspicious."

"Pardon me, sir, but Major Banks and I *shared* an office. Past tense."

He raised a white brow. "Oh?"

"Yeah, we stopped sharing an office three weeks ago as soon as one became available for her. The only reason we even shared one initially is because, of the two of us, I was the only one with an office here, and I didn't want to squish her down on the first floor with all the low ranks on our team."

"I see. So the rumors I've been hearing about her avoiding you aren't true. She just has her own office she works out of."

"Correct," I nodded with a smile… even though the rumors *were* true.

"Well, it wouldn't have mattered to me. Especially since you're basically the generals' secretary and she's yours. It would've been a secretary love story." He waggled his eyebrows.

I snorted. "Thanks for completely reducing my hard work."

General Hunter leaned back and laughed loudly for such a small older man. "Someone's got to do the work."

"Absolutely. I'm honored it's me," I said sarcastically.

The redness in his skin slowly dissipated as his laughter calmed. "I'm glad you've got a good personality, Claudius."

"Thank you, sir."

"Now, I've got something for you to do before I send you away."

"Fire away."

He nodded. "The Air Force, Marines, Navy, and the Guard are all bringing a slew of people tomorrow who'll need offices. So, I need you and Major Banks to go back to sharing an office and get the rest of your team into one office."

"The Guard? Why is everyone suddenly moving in?"

"Come on, General," he glanced around, lowering his voice as soldiers walked by, "you know better than I do that a war is here. It's not a matter of *if*, just when. Splitting coordination with Washington is going to require us to have more bodies here from the other branches. Just play nice."

I grunted. "As you wish."

"Very good." He smiled. "Now, don't let these guys being here mess with your focus. Screw the attitudes and keep your head low. There's a promotion waiting for you, so just do your job and don't tell anyone I told you all this."

I was ecstatic but did my best not to show it. I only had two more years as Brigadier General before having to retire.

Getting that promotion would give me another five years. I could finish this war out as a major general, which sounded good to me.

"Of course, sir." I saluted.

He gave me a dismissive nod, and I headed down the hall to Keoni's office. For a second, I was almost happy to see her when I remembered that we were still feuding. No matter what, we'd have to get over it soon, like *today* soon, since she had to move back in with me.

I slowed my pace to a stop, trying to think things over. What would I say? How do I apologize in a situation like this?

"General Olliare?" I turned to find a thin woman holding two folders under her arm as she munched on an apple.

"First Sergeant," I waved, "how are you?" She was one of the enlisted soldiers on my team. She was in charge of everyone beneath her rank, making sure the work got done correctly. She also reported to Keoni most days since our small team of sixteen didn't have a wide range of ranks.

I was allowed to pull a team together as my council, and as my hands. I needed advice, and I needed someone to do grunt work. I didn't really want advice, and Hunter knew that when he told me I could have my own team. He just wanted me to delegate some of the work to make sure it got done during these uncertain times.

"I'm good, sir, how are you?"

"Well. Is Major Banks in her office?" I asked.

"She is, actually. I was on my way to discuss these files with her. Would you like me to take a message?"

"No—actually—let me take those files to her and let her explain to me what's going on. You go back to the team and get them moved into a single office. You've got to move quick to get the biggest one you can find to fit all of you."

"May I ask why, sir?"

"The Guard and everyone else are coming in for good tomorrow. No more drop-ins. This *is* the joint force headquarters." I shrugged. However, my first sergeant looked bleak. Like she had just begun to understand the weight of the situation. Afraid she'd drift away in fear, I clapped and jolted her back to attention. She must've never seen war before.

"I need those folders."

"Yes, sir." She handed them to me before leaving.

With a big sigh, I turned and headed for Major Banks' office. When I finally made it to the door, I stood there staring at it. Then, with all the courage I could muster, I opened the door without knocking.

"Major Banks," I said as I stepped inside, "it's been hard to track you down for three weeks in one building."

Keoni was leaning against her desk. Her jacket was off, and she was eating spaghetti from a plastic container with one ankle crossed over the other. She looked relaxed. Well only for a split second upon entry. When she realized I'd entered her office without knocking, after three successful weeks of avoidance, she frowned fiercely.

"I'm on break, general. Is there something I can help you with?" she ground out.

"First Sergeant Yaz gave me these." I waved the folders. "She was on her way to discuss them with you, but I needed her to do a few things for me instead."

Keoni set her food on the desk and cleaned her hands on a paper towel before reaching for the folders. I placed my hand in hers and she snatched it away.

"Keoni, come on," I whined. "How long am I supposed to accept this treatment?"

"This is what you wanted. To be professional. I'm just doing what you want."

"Well now I want something else."

"Unfortunately, that's no longer possible. Can I please have the folders?"

"One mistake in retaliation to you sleeping with another man? Come on, Major Banks, you're not playing fair."

"*Playing fair?*" She crossed her arms over her chest, scowling like it was the only thing she knew how to do. "Do you seriously want to talk about playing fair?"

I groaned. Playing fair was a bad choice of words.

"Come on, Keoni," I pleaded again as I stepped closer to her. "We both made a mistake, let's just let it go."

"I'm trying!" she snapped, then she turned away and rested her hands on the desk as the silence ticked by. "I was so angry at myself; I was hoping you could overlook what I'd done. I thought I'd return, and you'd be the snarky and sarcastic general you'd always been. But you were just as angry with me as I was with myself."

I came and stood beside her. The walls around the room weren't decorated, but that was just like Keoni. I wasn't surprised in the least bit by her bare walls.

"I wanted to be the guy you were expecting when you came in, but I couldn't. For an entire year, I missed you. And when I had you back, I was afraid you were really gone. I've always come back, but you've never taken the chance to leave. And you didn't, yet again."

"I could never leave you, Claudius." She stood upright, her gaze meeting mine.

My hand moved to hers—and a knock came to the door.

"Come in," Keoni said. She didn't release my hand right away, her gaze lingering on mine before the door opened and we became boss and subordinate again.

"Major Banks," Whitney said, then she glanced at me and offered a quick smile. "General Olliare, I'm glad you're here."

That was a lie. It was written all over her face. Whitney and I had history, obviously. She was cute, red hair and pretty eyes. Whitney was the type of girl you'd bring home to your parents to convince them that you haven't thrown your life away. However, Keoni Banks? She was the type of *woman* you brought home when you were serious about marriage, about the next level. That was the stark difference between the two. Whitney may have outranked Keoni, but she certainly didn't outwit her.

"Colonel Whitney, what brings you by?" Keoni asked kindly. She was well aware of the history between Whitney and me, but she has never had much to say about it.

"Well, actually, I couldn't get in contact with the general," she nodded at me, "so I came here to ask you to pass a message along."

"What is it?" I asked.

"The draft notices are ready. We just got them from Washington. They want to branch out from Missouri and Washington first, then New York, Mississippi, Nevada, and California. And every quarter, the list will go out again to a few more states until we've covered them all." Keoni, though I knew she had no idea the draft notices had even been discussed, only offered Lieutenant Colonel Whitney a hand to receive the documents.

"The General and I will discuss this matter in private. I'll have these documents returned to you with any notes before the day is over."

"Excellent," Whitney said as she passed Keoni the papers. Her eyes flicked to mine for a moment before going back to Keoni.

"Well, if that was all. Whitney, you're dismissed," I said.

She stiffened. "Of course, general."

When the door closed, the papers in Keoni's hand struck the desk with a loud clap. "A draft? When were you going to tell me?"

"I tried," I flung my hands open, "but you were avoiding me!"

Rubbing her temples, she took a breath. "You could've sent an email, Ollie."

"I know but a draft is not an emailing matter. You know that."

She flopped into her chair. "People are going to be outraged. No one wants to be forced to fight for a country they don't believe in anymore."

I shook my head as I leaned against her desk. "No, people are more focused on their fear than patriotism. Which is why your job has been a dual position."

One of her eyebrows arched. "What am I? A drill sergeant again? I train soldiers at a high-ranking level, not new recruits who can't run a mile."

I leaned forward and swept away a loose curl that'd sprung free from her bun. "You're the best at all this stuff and you've got the purple heart to prove it."

"You mean I lost an eye and had to prove it," she said as she pushed my hand away. "What choice do I have?"

We both stood, and I shrugged. "Do you want me to lie or just give it to you straight?"

She smirked, picking up the papers from the desk and coming around the front of it. "Call Colonel Whitney," she said in a dark voice, "I'm sure she's waiting for you to give it to her straight." She shoved the papers into my chest and grabbed her keys off the desk.

"Aww, come on, Keoni. She's old news." I watched her cross the room to the door, where she stopped and looked over her shoulder at me.

"Now she's new news since she knew about the draft, and I didn't. Besides, I've got to head to the fields to train these kids at your request. Seems like I'm old news too."

"Kiki—"

She opened the door and left me in her office.

10

I Will Bring You Out

Keoni

Draft notices went out three weeks ago to men and women. The only exemptions were for members of the clergy ages thirty-five and higher, pregnant moms with up to three months postpartum, anyone over sixty-five was also exempt, and those with qualifying disabilities.

The age range was so wide for the draft because everyone from the Guard was being shifted to active duty, while older recruits were being put into office jobs for the Guard. There were also the younger recruits, seventeen to twenty, who would work as the active part of the Guard.

They'll be the ones handing out rations along with the police force and enforcing crowd control. Everyone twenty-one to forty-five will be joining as active-duty soldiers, but they'd also be 'on call.' That just meant they could head into the city to help with crowd control, but more than likely they'd be deployed.

Those who were operating as nonbinary, or something other than their birth gender were called to duty. Those with hormone changes would have exactly thirty days to begin weaning themselves from the hormones, while those with sex changes would be drafted as their birth gender. This, of course, caused a public outcry of discrimination and the military came under fire for our choices. However, in a time of desperation, selectivity was not an option.

I sighed as I watched two soldiers tackle a big man who'd been carrying a sign I didn't read, for the last two minutes out front of the joint force headquarters. Protesters have not only stormed Missouri, but they've stormed the capital as well. The lawn of the White House was filled with sex toys and signs that made a connection between genders being comparable to sex toys; *used for the government's pleasure*—or so the protesters said. They were blowing the whole thing out of proportion, considering everyone was sent draft notices, male *and* female.

"How's Jackson?" Ollie said with his feet on the desk.

I smacked his boots and sneered, "It's Jensen."

"When'd you start getting so protective?"

I rolled my eyes and sat on his couch. There were mounds of paperwork we had to go through for the new recruits. I hadn't been home much recently. It was starting to bother Jensen how much I was away, but with the draft notices I'd actually been busy. Not simply avoiding him.

Ollie pulled a few strings and Jensen's name was avoided for the draft. I hadn't asked him to do that. He decided he'd pull those strings on his own to make up for pulling rank on me before. No matter the reason, I couldn't deny my appreciation. I didn't want Jensen to be drafted for the sake of him staying out of military business. I was certain that if he'd been drafted, he'd have found out about Olliare and me, and we didn't need that.

"Are you excited for basic training?" Olliare's voice pulled me from my daydreams. He was leaning back in his chair, while his big sandy boots rested on the desk. Long legs, and a strong frame, Ollie kept his physique in good shape. Though his dark hair and square jaw made him attractive, the general was a man inching into his forties. He had deceptive green eyes that made you weak, and a youthful attitude and glowing skin. Ollie was a gentleman and lovely to talk to. He made for good company, humorous company.

"Not exactly." I sighed.

Normally, a drill sergeant wasn't an officer. Drill sergeants were usually enlisted soldiers who went through strenuous academy training. I was going to become a drill sergeant. I had been recommended for the academy after three years in the Guard, and I actually graduated from the National Guard's Drill Sergeant Academy.

However, I started taking classes since I was only training new recruits for a few weeks out of the year for the Guard and then I met Ollie, who pushed me to re-enlist as an officer. I've been qualified as the 'best of the best' in the Army National

Guard. Being a drill sergeant was one of the most rewarding and acknowledged positions in the military.

It meant you knew your branch better than even the guys up top, and it meant you excelled at combat. Which was exactly why, during a time of bubbling war, Ollie recommended me for the drill sergeant position. I didn't need schooling and I graduated at the number one seat in my class.

"Why not? Are you going to miss me so much?" Ollie teased.

I grunted. "I'm training these guys for the Army, not the Guard. There's a difference between the two."

"True, but you've got all the materials you need. You'll do fine, Keoni."

Rolling my eyes, I said, "I've got no choice."

He chuckled, pulling his feet from his desk as he moved to sit with me on the couch. "My little Kiki is going to be a drill sergeant again, and I'm going to be left here to do all the work by myself."

I pushed from the couch beside him, and his arm dropped into my seat. "I'm sure Colonel Whitney will have no problem filling in for me."

"Not this again," he said as he draped his arm over the top of the couch.

"I'm just saying. I noticed the way you two have been talking more, and it's actually a relief. I don't want to be away thinking of you, and not being focused on my duties."

"Keoni," he leaned his head back, "we have to work together. There's nothing more than that."

"Of course, general." I turned, my heart feeling weakened just by the mention of Whitney. I've never let Ollie's flings bother me in the past, but that was mostly because he never seemed close with anyone. A year apart had pushed us both into the arms of someone else. While I've had my fair share of happiness with Jensen, I should've expected the same for Ollie. Seeing him interacting with Whitney made me a little jealous, to say the least. However, I had no right to treat him poorly over it.

"*General?*" Ollie was sitting up now, arms still stretched out. "You're overreacting. You know me."

"I do." I crossed my arms, and he smirked.

He adjusted on the couch, his brow raised, a smirk across his face. "Come here."

Without hesitation, I followed orders. Each stride made my heart beat recklessly, and as I stood before him I thought the beating would be loud enough for him to hear. His eyes washed over me. He always said that in a sea of people wearing the same uniform, I always stood out.

He took a deep breath, finally sitting forward from the couch. He took my hands in his, pecking the top of each one, before pulling me closer. "Kiki," he whispered as he wrapped his arms around my waist, hugging me tightly.

I wrestled my fingers through his hair as he whispered how much he'd missed me. I would miss the general too, however, this war was bigger than the rekindling of our old flame. Besides, no matter how much I enjoyed Saint Ollie, I was still cheating on Jensen. It was wrong on so many levels, and if my

108

mother knew that not only was I shacking up, but now cheating on the guy I was living with… it's better to just focus on the moment with the general than think of that.

— ÷ —

"General Saint-Olliare and Major Banks, it's urgent."

I sat up immediately, rolling off of Ollie. He was still asleep on the couch, peaceful as if we weren't about to be caught. I decided against waking him, since both of us rushing around to dress would make too much noise and be too suspicious to the listening ears outside the door.

"One moment," I said sternly as I raced around the room to find my clothes. I tossed Ollie's jacket over him, and then his spare blanket. Tying my boots in record timing, I tucked my shirt in and zipped my jacket as I rushed to the door. Then I snatched a file off of Ollie's desk, I took a breath and pulled open the door.

"Captain Luther, what's the urgency?" I asked.

He squinted. "Where's the general?"

I glanced over my shoulder, and then looked back at Luther with my finger to my lips. "He's asleep."

"Right now? Aren't you two supposed to be working on formations?"

Thankfully, I'd grabbed the right folder that had the word 'formations' written across it, and I held it up. "We're actually done with these. I was just looking them over before putting General Saint Olliare's seal on them."

109

Luther wanted to frown, but there was nothing to be upset over. Though we weren't finished with the formations, Luther would never know that, and he wouldn't be able to ask any further questions, considering I was his superior.

"Well, major, please deliver the news that three of our soldiers have been captured by Chinese forces. And we want to send in a squad."

I blinked. "Send in a squad? For what? We need to pull everyone out, right now."

"They have our soldiers, major, we can't just leave them behind."

"You obviously don't understand war." I shook my head.

"Excuse me?"

"This isn't about the soldiers, captain," I stated.

Luther, indignant of my response fired, "You're willing to sacrifice people because you don't feel like dealing with it! You want to sit around here and snuggle up with Olliare. Well, let me tell you something, Keoni," Luther stepped forward, "me and you both know you only got this promotion because you're sleeping with the general. *I* deserved that promotion. And I am not going to let soldiers die because the wrong choice was made."

"Very good." I looked over my shoulder to find Ollie right behind me, clapping his large hands as he entered the doorway—completely dressed in his uniform. Not even a hair out of place.

"General," Luther stepped back and swallowed loudly, "I didn't know you were—"

110

"Here? In my own office?"

"Awake."

"So when my back is turned, this is how you talk to your superior?"

"No, sir, not at all."

Ollie stepped in front of me, glaring down at Luther who was trying to hold his gaze. "I chose Major Banks based on her skillset. I am a planner, I make decisions based on future possibilities, and I plan for the unknown. Major Banks was part of my plan for the unknown. We had no grounds to believe this invasion would turn into what it has." Ollie spoke calmly, not an ounce of anger in his voice. "However, in the case that it did turn into something bigger, Major Banks was chosen based on her past experience. You see that patch," he pointed to my eye patch, "she earned that by giving up her sight for the mission. Her dedication and loyalty will never be forgotten. Not by her, or anyone else she rescued that day."

"Sir, may I speak?"

"No," Ollie answered darkly. "If it wasn't for this uncertain time, you'd be demoted by now. However, since I can't demote you, I will remove you from top secret clearance." Ollie grabbed the door. "You're dismissed." He slammed it in Luther's bright red face, then turned to me with a sympathetic look. "He was disrespectful," he said before heading to his desk.

"You took away his top secret clearance. That sucks."

"He should be thankful I didn't make him turn in his papers!"

"Thank you for doing that."

He shrugged as he gripped the chair.

"We need to talk about what's going on. China has three soldiers of ours."

"You know we can't send a team in for three soldiers when we're trying to be stealthy. China is taunting us, and we cannot entertain this."

"Do you agree we should pull out?" I asked.

"No, but I do think we should hold off on sending more bodies in until we can either retrieve the taken soldiers with the teams on the ground, or until China's done taunting us."

"Whichever comes first," I said as I crossed my arms.

11

Into the Hand of Their Adversaries

Zion

Abigail had soft feet. I kissed each one before massaging them. She giggled the whole time, pleading with me to stop, but secretly enjoying it. Abbey and I were close again, and everything felt right. We decided to keep the baby and do the right thing. Marriage wasn't exactly on or off the table, which was horrible, I know. But a baby was one thing, adding marriage into the mix was a whole different story.

I didn't know if I was ready for that, though I knew my mother would tell me otherwise. She'd say something along the lines of, *'If you're ready to lay down and get what you want despite the possibilities, then you should be ready to stand at the altar despite the responsibilities.'*

"Have you picked out a name yet?" I asked as I continued to massage Abbey's feet. They were small and soft, and her toes were painted a girly pink color.

"I'm not sure yet. I want our little girl to have the perfect name."

"Me too." I nodded.

"You don't care." She laughed.

"I do." I kissed the top of her foot. "I care about our daughter." I leaned forward and began kissing up her slender legs. "And I care about you." Her laughter became shy as I crawled onto the bed and pecked her exposed belly in her cropped shirt before reaching up and kissing her lips. "And I care about us."

"And Jala? What about her?" Abigail asked.

"What about her? It's me and you now." I leaned down and kissed her again. "No one else matters."

She smiled, reaching up to touch my cheek. Her brown eyes were filled with happiness as she leaned forward and kissed me. "Do you love me, Zion?"

"Of course, I do."

"I want to hear you say it. Tell me you love me."

"I love you, Abigail. And I love our daughter already."

"Zion, I—"

The doorbell rang and Abbey didn't get to finish her sentence. I crawled off the bed and shooed her to the guestroom to hide. She'd stopped staying there two weeks ago, when I snuck into her room at night. No one knows she's here. My parents think I'm always home now because I want time alone from them since we're doing more church functions, and community events with the world hanging by a thread.

I left the bedroom and headed for the door. When the bell rang again, I took a deep breath, and hoped it wasn't my father. He was the only person impatient enough not to wait for a response from me.

"One moment," I called as I grabbed the door and pulled it open.

To my surprise, it was a man in a military uniform. Not the normal digital fatigues, he was dressed in his military suit. The dark blue jacket with gold accents, and a ton of ribbons on his chest. His shoes shined as I swept him over in one quick look.

"Can I help you?" I asked.

"Are you Zion Reinhardt?"

"Who's asking?"

"The United States Military."

"What... What is this about?" I clutched the door as I took a deep breath.

"We were asked to hand deliver your draft notice. You have been selected for the Army National Guard's draft. You will be serving in the Guard until called into active duty. Basic training begins in two weeks. Please have your affairs in order by then." He extended the letter to me, and with a shaky hand, I took it from him.

"I'm... I'm a member of the clergy. I'm not supposed to be drafted." I swallowed dryly, like my entire world had just been turned upside down. "This must be a mistake." I looked up from the letter at the soldier, but his uncaring eyes and

115

unmoved demeanor told me this was all but a mistake. Why would my letter be hand delivered?

"Members of the clergy aged thirty-five and over are exempt. If you have any more questions, please reference the letter. Have a good evening." He nodded and excused himself as I stood there with my hands trembling.

Being drafted meant I was going to see war, no matter how long it took. And it also meant war was coming if it wasn't already here.

"Baby?" Abbey's gentle call pulled me from my sinking thoughts of despair.

Slowly closing the door, I stood there just breathing as I stared down at the white envelope in my hands. **Zion Reinhardt**, my name was printed on the back in bold black letters.

"Zion…" Abbey's hand on my back made me jump.

She took a step when I turned to her, her eyes darting over me in concern until she spotted the letter in my hand. "What is that?"

"It's a letter," I forced out. My eyes couldn't stop focusing on my name printed on the back.

I had been drafted. Was this some kind of joke? Was this some kind of punishment from God? Why was this happening?

"What kind of letter?" I could hear the concern in Abigail's voice shifting to fear.

"It's a draft notice."

Her hands went to her mouth as her big eyes misted instantly. "What?"

"I got drafted, Abbey. What am I supposed to do?" I glanced down at her belly. "We can't have a kid now."

"What?" One of her small hands fell to her belly, and she backed up. "Zion, hold on. We can't just jump to conclusions. What if this is wrong?"

"And what if it isn't? You can't raise a kid alone or you never would've come back here. And you can't raise a kid during the war, Abbey."

"I'm not having this conversation again." She shook her head, walking backwards down the hall. When I didn't reply, she turned away and headed into the bedroom.

I sighed, raking a hand through my hair. I didn't bother opening the letter. I tucked it under my arm and went for the door, grabbing my shoes and car keys on the way out. I didn't even grab a jacket, despite the chill outside.

I barely pulled the car into the driveway before hopping out and banging on my parents' door.

"Open up!" I called from outside. I banged again, the way my heart banged against my chest.

I can admit I was afraid to go to war, but I was angry too. I'd been drafted despite what my father told me about pulling strings so I wouldn't ever face this situation.

Why did the president, my father's old friend, change his mind about me?

"Mom! Dad! Open the doo—"

"Zion?" my mother snapped as she ripped open the door. I would've liked to have taken a moment to acknowledge my mother's strength since she snatched open a grand oak door with one hand, but I had more pressing issues. "Zion, what are you doing banging on the door like that?" she asked in a firm, mother's voice.

"This." I held up the letter, but my mother's dark eyes only squinted.

"What is it?" She took the envelope and walked into the house as I stepped inside behind her.

I watched her open the letter in silence as I kicked the door shut behind me and waited. What was once an annoyed glare, was now a shocked expression. My mother never expected this, considering the president himself had promised I'd be safe from the draft.

Raised brows, and wide-open eyes, I thought my mother would snap right that moment and just scream. But she was stronger than that. Passing the letter back to me, she said, "Let me get your father. Have a seat."

I nodded and headed for the front room as my mother's shocked demeanor sank into the floor with every calm step she took towards the stairs. I think my mother had to be calm because she knew my father wasn't going to be. He'd probably throw a fit, yell and shout, and then call President Warrick. But my mother would be able to keep his anger contained to some degree. She'd also be the one giving logical advice until my father calmed down.

Jillian's footsteps thudded down the stairs as I waited in the living room. When my father rounded the corner, his eyes were set ablaze, and he didn't mutter a word as he snatched the letter from me. In the tense silence, he read the letter to himself. His blue eyes darted around the paper as he flushed red.

"I knew it," he whispered through clenched teeth. "I knew it was Roger." In an instance, he whirled around to face my mother who was standing in the archway. "It's the Secretary of Defense, Roger Donald! He signed this along with Warrick, who signs all the notices. Warrick probably doesn't even know this went to Zion."

"A man in uniform came and delivered it himself. He said he was told to hand deliver my letter."

"Hand deliver it?"

"Yes." I nodded, understanding that the method of delivery made all the difference to my father. If this had been a swearing household, my father would have unleashed a string of words that would've scared the devil. Instead, he released a very slow sigh and muttered, "Give me strength…" I didn't have to ask Who he wanted strength from.

"Did you tell him that you were a member of the clergy?" my mother asked as my father turned to leave. He tromped across the room in a fit of anger but stopped abruptly when I said, "Yes, but he told me clergy members must be thirty-five years old to be exempt from the draft."

Jillian Reinhardt was stunned as he stood there with tense muscles in his face and all over. The paper crinkled in his hand as he grinded out, "I'm going to call Fallon right now." Without another word, my father turned on his heels and left the room.

"That age range, it blocks young people from joining the clergy. Most drafts want young strong soldiers, so if they can keep the young ones available, they will," Mom explained as she sat beside me.

"But I'm *actually* a member of the clergy, and I have been for years now."

"I know, which is why this is particularly hard for your father."

"I don't understand."

She adjusted beside me, brushing her hair from her face. "Receiving a draft notice behind the president's back is one thing. But the age restriction is another thing. The terms of the draft are signed and approved by the president."

I let go of an exhausted sigh. "That means President Fallon was well aware of my age and status and signed this into law without any exemptions."

Mom gave me a nod, and we sat in silence as I thought it all over. If Dad couldn't fix this, I would be leaving for basic training in two weeks. According to the letter, basic training was three months straight and would be in conjunction with something called, 'Advanced Individual Training.' Supposedly the AIT and the bootcamp would be a miniature version, just enough training to get us ready for war. And after three months of training, we'd be spending four-day weekends in our specified division, but we won't know which division we're getting into until after graduating from bootcamp.

Dad came down the stairs, his loud footsteps drew me from the thoughts I'd been swamped in as Mom and I sat in silence. His thundering steps told me that my fate had been sealed. Mr. President hadn't answered, I assumed. But it wasn't until my mother grabbed my hand, and I saw tears in her eyes that I knew that two weeks was all I had before my life would change forever.

— ÷ —

I had been right, President Fallon didn't answer when my father called last week, and he hadn't answered at all this week either. My father was being ignored by his old friend while I steadily prepared for bootcamp.

"I leave in the morning," I said to Abbey. She was sitting on the edge of our bed with a tired look on her face. We'd argued all last week about her getting an abortion. She'd refused, and honestly, I just didn't care anymore.

I didn't care if I offended Abbey or God at this point. He'd stopped looking out for me a while ago anyway. I couldn't even be mad at Him—because I felt nothing towards Him now.

I didn't want to pray. I didn't want forgiveness. I just wanted to be left alone, the way He'd left me for years now. I'd tried many times to do the right thing, but I guess I was the one He forgot to put His righteousness in. Who knows? I can't even say I believe the words I've been saying to myself. It's

121

more like, I'm so disappointed, so hurt. Maybe if I'd gotten things right with God sooner, I wouldn't have been drafted. Was this truly His punishment? Sending me to the frontlines?

"Three months is a long time," Abbey said as she rubbed her belly.

"Would you stop it?" I snapped standing by the dresser.

"Stop what?"

"Rubbing your belly. It's annoying."

"You've got to be kidding me." She stood from the bed. Her lace robe fell open, revealing her cocoa brown belly poking out. She was walking to the door when I hopped over my open suitcase and caught her by the wrist. Brooding eyes narrowed on me with an intense anger she was trying to control.

"I'm sorry," I said politely. "It's all so much on me right now."

Her gaze began to soften, and she sighed. "Zion, it's just as much for me as it is for you. I can't be your emotional punching bag every time you get stressed. And I can't let my daughter's life hang in the air every time you're uncertain about something."

My brows furrowed as I squinted at her. "Are you leaving me?"

"No." She shook her head. "But I am telling you that when you return, our daughter will only be a few weeks away from birth. Which means there's no more second guessing this, Zion. While you're away, you need to accept that we're having a child. And if you can't, then I'll disappear just like I promised."

Abigail was right. I couldn't do this to her anymore. I couldn't confuse myself anymore either. Using these three months to clear my head and get things right with God— though I had proclaimed to no longer want to know Him— and accept that I'm having a kid was sound advice. This was going to happen, no matter what. I couldn't keep flip-flopping. Maybe space was all I ever needed to accept this; I won't know until I get there.

"Alright, Abbey. I'll take this time to figure things out," I promised her.

She nodded and gave me a small smile.

"Will you wait for me then?" I asked. "And take care of my place?"

"Yes." Carefully, she wrapped her arms around my neck, and I pulled her as close as I could, despite the baby bump.

"I... I love you, Abigail." I surprised myself when I spoke. But her assuring response made me feel like all the abrupt changes in my life happening at once would all be okay.

"I love you too."

12

I Am Against You

Claudius

"General." Whitney nodded as I entered the boardroom. She was going to be a replacement for the next three months until Keoni returned. I missed my major already, but I was busy enough to forget about her.

There'd been word that some soldiers had found the location of the Chinese hideout where our men were being held hostage. The board meeting today would discuss the best course of action regarding that information.

"Evening, Whitney. Why's the Guard here again?" I muttered before taking a seat. She passed me a smile before grabbing her own chair beside me at the table. I glanced Whitney over before looking around the room at the other branches, trying to stay focused.

The US was in hot waters. For now, I couldn't let any other thoughts into my head. Not about my past with Whitney and not about the present with Keoni. I'd promised Keoni my loyalty which made her paranoid that I'd be unruly while she was gone. In all actuality, I desperately wanted to hold on to Keoni. I was even considering retiring once I got my promotion so that I could marry Ms. Banks. But that's a story for another day.

As I glanced around, I realized there was nothing but colonels, generals, a few sergeant majors, and other high-ranking leaders from every branch. The stuffy room filled with sacks of old people in starched uniforms made me want to squirm. However, I knew that being included in this meeting was an honor. Top secret clearance wasn't handed out to just anyone. Being included in war plans meant that somewhere in history, you wouldn't be forgotten. I loved that.

There was a screen set up at the end of the long brown table where I assumed the folks from Washington would be tuning in. This was only my third time in one of these virtual meetings. The president had been present once, and I was certain he'd be present again today.

Unfortunately for me, I wouldn't get to just sit back and watch like I usually did. I'd have to participate, and we'd have to make a decision about the lives of soldiers, which was never easy.

"Saint Olliare." Hunter slapped my shoulder. "I didn't think you'd accept the invite."

I stood, nodding at him. "Sir, I wasn't sure I could refuse."

He snorted. "You know you could've. You love this stuff, no matter how much you say you hate it." We shook hands and he grabbed a seat closer to the head of the table. Those with higher ranks sat at the head. Normally, if it was just the Army, I'd be closer to the front, however, with all the branches under a single roof, I was comfy sitting at the center of the table with Whitney.

"Now that everyone's here," General Collins said, "I'll be connecting us to Washington. Standby."

The screen flickered on a few seconds later; a table and room set up as a replica of ours held a large number of normal looking people, beside the few decorated Commandants, Chiefs, and other military personnel. There were only a few Admirals, most of them were present here at our table, but the Fleet Admiral was on screen in Washington.

Right away, I found the Secretary of Defense, Roger Donald, sitting beside President Warrick Fallon.

"Good morning, everyone," Roger started. "We are here today because of the intel recently received about soldiers finding the hideout where their fellow men are being held hostage. Today we need to make a decision in regard to this matter. And the president has made a special request; he would like to involve the military branches in a few international decisions. He thinks it's best to include the people who will be fulfilling the missions."

"We appreciate that," General Collins spoke. If things continued to escalate, which we all knew they would, General Collins would be selected for the General of the Army, and

126

he'd be shipped to Washington while all of us would get a promotion.

The General of the Army was a special honor, only given during war, and I couldn't think of a man more dedicated to the military and more deserving of that rare title than Collins. He'd been a real leader, one I'd looked up to before I became a general. And when I finally met the guy, he turned out to be absolutely normal, which was great.

"I would like to begin with the foreign aid issue," the president spoke gruffly. He was a lanky man, silver hair and small eyes that always looked empty.

Roger glanced at the president, but only nodded. There was an uncomfortable shift in the room. As soldiers sat around, many who'd seen combat, putting our brothers on the back burner to discuss foreign aid didn't sit too well with any of us. However, President Fallon had always been an unusual man. A little quirky, and maybe a little too old to be doing this job.

"Ms. Coga, our Secretary of State, will give us information on the international affairs."

The camera zoomed in on a small woman who was now standing. She wore a blazer with an American flag pin on it, paired with a knee-length skirt. Adjusting the glasses on the tip of her wrinkly nose, she read aloud from a paper, "According to the Security Coordinator of Israel and the surrounding nations, Israel has no movement from the ships who've been sitting on the Mediterranean Sea, or the Gulf of Aqaba. However, there's been an increase in foot traffic at the northern border of Israel."

"What does that mean?" an admiral seated across from me asked with a raised hand.

"It means people have been near the border, selling at the border—whatever they do at the Israeli border—it's increased," Ms. Coga explained.

"Well, an increase in movement doesn't mean we need to be there," the Secretary of Defense said curtly.

"I differ on that," Collins spoke.

The president gave him a nod, and the general continued, "Israel is clearly going to be invaded, the same way Taiwan was. Should we wait, like we did with Taiwan, until it's too late and have to scramble? Or should we just put a plan together now? Get troops over there and weapons."

"General Collins, I believe it was your signature at the bottom of a report that suggested we split aid between Israel and Taiwan, though there wasn't much to split."

"Yes," Collins agreed with Roger, "however, sir, we're getting more soldiers prepared now. We have the capabilities to help both areas."

"We may have bodies, but they won't be well trained. Not like regular soldiers, they're getting just a taste of bootcamp."

"General Collins," I raised my hand. He glanced back at me, relieved that someone would come to his aid. "May I speak, sir?"

"You may."

The attention was now on me, and I realized I was an idiot. I was only speaking up on the new recruits because Keoni was a drill sergeant, and I knew she would train and make some very qualified soldiers.

"Just to touch on the training, Mr. Secretary, we have some of the most skilled and qualified drill sergeants training these draftees. And the program we have the new soldiers working through is a combination of bootcamp and the Advanced Individual Training which most soldiers fulfill in four to fifty-two weeks, a few days after bootcamp. We've broken down the components of the AIT to fit the three specialized programs each candidate will test into."

"Go on," the president urged.

"We have special forces, taught by a former Green Beret and a current Ranger. The soldiers will be tested to see which of these two special forces groups they would excel in." I glanced over at Collins who was smiling proudly before I continued. "Of course, we know the training for these elite groups is daunting and not everyone makes it through. For those who don't complete the special forces training, or didn't test into it, they'll have the option of becoming a canon crew member, or an infantry man. Both of which are heavily needed."

"So, I take it you're saying that we'll have well-trained or elite soldiers?" Roger asked.

"Yes, sir."

"Well that only solves one problem. We still have resources—that's a problem. We're short, and we can't get anything from Europe because they've been had."

"What do you mean?" someone around the table asked what we were all thinking.

"The King of England, as we know, united nearly all of Europe together during the famine. His methods included working with the Islamic Brotherhood who is associated with members of the Taliban. And those Taliban members are receiving aid from China. So, down the pipeline," Ms. Coga sighed, "Europe cannot help us or they're violating their treaty with the Brotherhood, and the Brotherhood will be violating their agreement with China."

"How many more nations are tied up like that?" Admiral Zhao asked. China's attack on Taiwan made things personal for the admiral. He was Chinese American and had family in China that he was no longer allowed to speak to or visit since the invasion. He'd been handling the disconnection well, though I knew he was worried.

"Too many," Roger said. "It's like during the five years of peace, China went around collecting our allies with a ten-foot spoon. Using their secret allied forces to swindle countries into deals. They fed everyone and supplied needs around the world to get to this moment," Roger spoke harshly. "They made a fool of us!"

We all knew it, but no one wanted to speak about it. The US had been wounded by viruses, a mountain of debt, and a loss of patriotism. And the famine was everything we didn't need. However, with China owning farmland in our country, particularly *rich* farmland, and farmland around the world, they became the superpower we'd been trying to stay afloat as.

There was silence over who ruled the world during the famine. However, when the world's economy began to stabilize again, China's kindness had not been forgotten. No one thought they'd turn their backs on the world. But they could now that they had the world in their hand.

In the silence, the black phone sitting in the center of the table rang. It would only ring for one reason, because it was only linked to one team.

General Collins' eyes widened as he glanced up at the screen.

"Answer it," the president said.

Snatching up the phone, he pressed a button and set the receiver down. "It's live, sir—"

White noise rang out before the sound of heavy breathing and gunfire went off.

"Sir! We're here! We're here! Permission to enter, sir!?" There was a soldier on the opposite end, radioing us. They'd gotten the communication crew out there to rewire one of the radios to connect to our phone line so we could speak with the team moving in on the Chinese hideout.

"What's your position?" General Collins called. He was now acting as the General of the Army, calling shots on behalf of Washington when needed and all of the US Army.

"We're just north of the Strait, sir!" a soldier replied. "We can confirm that our soldiers are in there!"

A whistling noise pierced the phone and more white noise rang out.

"Come in! Sergeant Downey, come in!"

"We... eyes on... they have...! Permission— ... Sir!?"

"Hold your position!" Collins yelled back before hitting the mute button. He turned to the screen. "Mr. President. They have eyes on the target is what I'm picking up from this. Please, those are our comrades, we cannot leave those soldiers behind when we are so close."

"If they go in there, they are going to let all of China know we aren't pulling out!" a man in a marine's uniform shouted.

"We aren't pulling out," Roger confirmed, "but we do need the element of surprise. Are three soldiers worth losing everything we've been building up?"

"Are you serious?" I snapped. "That's ridiculous. China is taunting us, and you know it. We should grab those soldiers and retreat. Pull out now. We let China know we aren't afraid of them and let that be the end of it."

"Please," Vice Admiral Zhao waved a hand, "China isn't going to let this go if we go in there. We should completely retreat."

"We can't leave them," General Collins pressed.

"And we can't save them either," the Secretary of Defense said.

"But we can save Taiwan?" I bunched my shoulders. "Does that make sense?"

"If we go in there, we're going to lose the element of surprise and turn our aid to Taiwan into a full-blown war for ourselves." Roger tried to keep his temper from flaring as he spoke.

General Hunter was about to chime in when the phone released a high-pitched sound before screams and shots filled the entire room.

"Sergeant Downey!" Collins was hollering now. "Downey, come in!"

"We're moving in! We can't wait any longer!"

"No! No! No!" Roger shouted. "Tell them to retreat!"

"Downey!" Collins looked wary, like he didn't want to say it. However, he swallowed his own desires and complied. "Retreat! Downey, retreat!"

Foreign language, and gunfire went off. No one was listening to Collins any longer. Collins stood frozen over the phone, listening to the screams and cries, listening to the beginning of one of the most anticipated wars of the century; the United States versus China. The phone line went dead after an explosion, and the eerie silence that followed made my ears feel like they were numb.

Quietly, Collins replaced the receiver and sat down.

"We are going to war," Ms. Coga said quietly. The light reflecting off her glasses made her statement seem even more mystifying.

"Admirals, get the fleets together," President Fallon began. He looked determined while his counterpart, Roger Donald, looked defeated. "We need air support, and land support. General Collins, you will be promoted to General of the Army this evening. We'll have a virtual ceremony before you fly out in the morning. We'll make the arrangements."

"Y-yes, sir. Thank you, sir, for the honor."

He nodded. "For the rest of you, get things in order. We need operations, intel, and whatever else we need to gather in order to be prepared for China's strike. And one last thing," the president said, "pull all resources from Israel, Palestine, Chad, and wherever else you can."

"Sir," Ms. Coga spoke up, "Israel needs us."

"The US is about to fight its strongest opponent ever. Israel doesn't need our help. And if they do later, then we'll cross that bridge when we get to it. And that's final."

Somewhere in my soul, I knew pulling resources from Israel was a grave mistake. One that could cost us more than we can gain from the pulled resources.

13

You Will Advance

Keoni

"Let's go!" I shouted at the draftees as they raced from the bus. In their standard fitness uniform, black bottoms and a top with the word 'Army' written in gold, and their freshly shaven heads, the draftees reminded me of my time in bootcamp.

I had always been weak. Weak minded, weak spirited, and physically weak. But, after high school with nothing to do because I wasn't too smart and didn't get a good enough scholarship for college, I joined the Army. I was too afraid to join the Marines and didn't know enough about the other branches to join. I wanted to get stronger, to be tougher, and it didn't hurt that I'd have a paying job that kept me away from my poor upbringing.

My mother, a single mom of seven, did her best with us. Four girls, three boys; I was the youngest out of all seven, but

135

I happen to think I made my mother the proudest. At least work wise. My two older sisters and one of my brothers went to church with my mother regularly, so I know she dotes on them regardless of their job status.

When I joined the military almost nine years ago, I joined the Army National Guard. If I'd known then just how decorated my career was going to be, I would've never believed it. I spent my first three years on the Guard as a part timer who was also going to school. That's when I met Ollie, but we didn't get serious right away. Eventually though, once Ollie and I started seeing each other, I stopped taking classes when I turned twenty-one. I was accepted into the special forces program and graduated as a Green Beret a year later.

I went on two missions as a Green Beret; a trip to Africa to train an elite group in their military with diverse combat operations, and my second mission was in Ukraine, when I lost my eye. As a Green Beret, you need to be in tip top shape, and with a missing eye, my body was no longer in perfect shape.

I was a good Beret. The little girl from the hood who was a weakling had become a Green Beret for one year, but that was snatched from me when I lost my eye. I should've been honorably discharged, however, I refused and proved to myself and everyone else that I was just as strong, if not stronger, without my eye.

Some rules cannot be broken, no matter how strong you are or how much stronger you become. My fighting spirit did impress my superiors, and I wasn't discharged. I was a special case and was recommended to become a drill sergeant. I only worked part time as a drill sergeant for the Army National Guard for two years while I went back to school.

That was when Ollie told me to go active and I reenlisted as an officer. With my schooling and expertise, I was promoted to first lieutenant. Of course, as a parting gift six months later, Ollie got me promoted to captain. I'd still be a captain if this tension hadn't become a war and there wasn't a vacancy that needed to be filled in the major spot. My life in the Army had been a rare and special case, but I was thankful for it.

As I watched the draftees line up, holding their bags above their heads, I wondered just how many of them would have a special story like mine. Considering we were not only training these draftees to go active duty, but we were also training them to go into special forces, infantry, or canon crews. Everyone was going to double up, the same way I had when I joined the Army.

We had basic training at the same time as our Advanced Individual Training school since I was going in for infantry. However, this program these draftees would be going through was a concentrated AIT schooling that would give them a little bit of everything to prepare them for their specialized training. As the war rages daily, time is of the essence and training needed to be done quickly and efficiently.

The draftees clutched their bags above their heads as they waited for commands. It was one of the first training exercises every recruit completed. I remembered doing the same thing and remembered holding this same exercise when I first became a drill sergeant.

"Listen closely," I said as I stepped forward. "All of you are technically official members of the United States Army because you have no choice but to graduate or die. If you are injured, we will wait for you to heal up and bring you back in." I shrugged. "So try to stay healthy."

The other drill sergeants laughed as I went on.

"You all are training for war. America needs you; your families and friends need you. People you've never even met need you and are depending on you for protection. So, I want you to pull out your phones. Text and call anyone you need to and let them know you'll contact them when you can because you are training to save the nation."

Weeks went by, and the new recruits were shaping up to be good soldiers. The days were grueling, but they made the most of them. I hadn't spoken much to Ollie or Jensen, but I hadn't expected to. Being out in the fields, the signals were shabby at best, and by the time my days were over, I was too exhausted to talk anyway.

Drill sergeants were up by 3AM to do their own personal training and then get showered and ready for the recruits by 5AM. Every day was split into class sessions and platoon training.

Today, the recruits were working more on their marksmanship. My favorite exercise was gun disassembling.

"Check your weapons," I called as I stood at the front of the class. "Make sure they are locked and loaded."

"Always loaded, Drill Sergeant!" the class responded together.

"Knowing your weapon is the key to every battle. Knowing how much pressure you need to apply on the trigger. Knowing what's wrong when your weapon doesn't fire correctly. Most times in battle you have a split second to swap to a secondary weapon." I walked the lines of the soldiers in their uniforms putting their rifles together. The digital green patterns against the pristine white floors the draftees cleaned and waxed made them all look like real soldiers.

"You need to be able to count your rounds while firing and focusing," I said loudly. "If for some reason your gun doesn't fire or has some strange problem on the battlefield, that's when you switch to your secondary. But you must have the awareness to know something's not right and to switch. It's really not hard." I shrugged. "But you can easily…" my words trailed off as I made it to the end of a row of soldiers. There was a guy sitting back there who instantly made me miss Ollie.

He was stunning. However, his tan skin and dark hair with a piercing blue gaze wasn't what stopped me. It was his nonchalance as he looked up at me, as if wondering why I had stopped in front of him.

"I've seen you around," I said hotly. "What's your name, soldier?"

"Reinhardt, Drill Sergeant."

"Why aren't you working, Reinhardt?"

139

"Because I finished putting my rifle together, Drill Sergeant."

"Did I tell you to stop?"

"No, Drill Sergeant."

"You've got two minutes left in class. What would you do on the battlefield if you were two minutes away from invading enemy territory? Would you sit there like it's a summer afternoon? Or would you be checking your weapons?"

"Checking my weapons, Drill Sergeant."

I glanced at my watch. "You've got exactly sixty seconds to disassemble and put your weapon back together. Starting now. Everyone else, you're dismissed."

I stood there with my arms crossed as I watched this Reinhardt soldier take his weapon apart. Fifteen seconds had already passed, and he hadn't even separated the receiver from the top. He was pushing down with his ammo on the back pin, but it wouldn't come loose.

"Do you see why it's important to always check your weapon? What if something was wrong with the bolt carrier and you needed to fix it quickly on the battlefield?" I asked.

"I wouldn't be able to do it," he said softly.

I sighed as I reached for his weapon. "When you put it back together, you forced it together instead of making everything line up. That's the problem." I gave the weapon a thump and tried pressing that pin again. It popped loose. "I want you to disassemble and reassemble this weapon until I get back. And when I return, I want you to be able to take the rifle

140

apart and put it together again in sixty-five seconds. Understood?"

"Yes, Drill Sergeant." He nodded as I passed the gun back to him. I didn't bother to stay to give him any further directions. I took the time to make a few phone calls. One to Jensen and then one to Ollie.

Pushing open my office door, I kicked it closed as I dialed Jensen's number.

"Hello?" He picked up on the second ring.

"Hey, Jenny."

"Hey, Keoni, you finally called. I was hoping you would this week."

"Is something going on?" I asked as I walked around the office to my chair.

"Well, actually, yeah."

I stopped. Jensen never really had anything going on. He could be breaking up with me, which wouldn't hurt me, just surprise me.

"I'm glad I called then."

"Me too." He paused. "I'm joining the police force."

"What? What about your accounting dreams?"

"I'm glad you remember that." He laughed. "Honestly, Ki, I think I'm suited for this. I want to stand beside you, not *behind* you, like I always have."

I rolled my eyes as I sat on my desk. "Why didn't you join the Army then?"

"Because I can handle people. But not war. And anyone who joins the force before the cutoff date won't be drafted."

141

"I didn't know they were doing something like that."

"Yeah, we need police just as much as soldiers right now."

The urge to say 'I doubt it' was like a tongue of fire burning my mouth. "Well, I'm here at basic training for another four weeks. You'll have made up your mind by then, won't you?"

"I'm sorry. I wish you could be here for this."

"Me too," I said patiently. Jensen and I had just been going through the motions lately. It was painfully obvious that there was distance between us but neither of us wanted to address it. My pride and guilt were in the way, and his gentleness kept him from asking why I'd been so distant. "Just promise me," I said in the awkward silence, "that you'll be careful, alright?"

"I promise, Ki. I love you."

"I love you too."

We hung up and I sighed in relief. I wondered if Jensen had sighed too. Dragging things out with him only made things harder on me. It was better to just rip the bandage off and be done with it. But I just didn't have it in me. I guess in some respects, I was still that weak girl from the ghetto.

With another sigh, I dialed Ollie's number. He'd been caught up with office work, we hadn't had much time to talk.

"Hello? Kiki?"

"Hi, Ollie." I could feel myself smiling.

"Kiki, come home already!" He sighed into the phone.

I laughed. "There's only four more weeks, general. You'll be fine."

"Yeah, but I miss you like crazy."

"I miss you too."

"How are things there?"

"Good, for the most part. I've got a rookie in the other room doing disassembling exercises by himself. He was wasting time in the back of class."

"Oh goodness, I don't know how any of the rookies are surviving with you."

I waved a hand, though he couldn't see it. "I'm nicer to them since they've got so much more training to do now."

"You? Nice? Please," he laughed, "Kiki, sweetheart, you're hardly nice to me."

"You've gotta be kidding me?" I joked.

"Man, your little giggle is so cute over the phone. I wish you were here right now. Things are bad out there."

"Worse than before?"

"I haven't told you everything that happened after the men moved in on the Chinese hideout."

"What haven't you told me?"

"That we're in an all-out naval war, and just last week China sank two of our ships. They're using our fleets to invade Taiwan but using little speed boats to fight us. They're darting around the waters at a much faster pace than we are, with less equipment and more accuracy."

"It's like they were prepared for this," I said as I bit my lip. "Ollie, what is really going on?"

"I have no idea. It all feels like a setup, doesn't it?"

"Yeah. But this isn't the end goal."

"No, there's definitely something more to it."

"Major Banks? You in here?"

"Hold on, Ollie." I covered the phone with my hand and glanced at the door. "Yes, in here!"

A familiar face peeked inside. "Hey, Banks, there's a rookie out here working on his gun. He says he's with you."

"Yeah, I stepped away to make a phone call."

Davis waved. "No matter. I'll take him off your hands now."

"Really? Thanks."

He nodded. "Of course, major."

When the door closed, I raised the phone back to my ear. "Ollie."

"I'm here. Listening to another man take care of you."

"Oh, stop it." I laughed as I hopped off the desk and slipped into my chair.

"Listen, Kiki, when you get back, I've got a little surprise for you."

I chewed my lip, trying to resist the urge to squeal. "Really? What kind of surprise?"

"The kind I think will make you smile, and make you like me a little more," he teased.

"I don't think I can like you any more than I already do, sir."

His chuckle sounded tired over the phone. "I love when you call me sir. It sounds kind of—"

"General Saint-Olliare," I cut him off, "I'd better go."

"Already?"

"Yes. We're not supposed to be on the phone anyways."

"While you were gone, I got promoted, Kiki."

144

"What? Why didn't you tell me?" I sat forward in surprise.

"I wanted it to be a surprise because of what was to follow. But the plans have changed now, and I can't walk away."

"What do you mean?"

"Well," I could hear him shifting around. "After getting promoted I was going to retire, but I think I'm still needed here."

"Retire? Ollie, are you feeling alright?"

"Perfect actually. I was going to retire for you. I wanted to give you the life and the love you deserved. I was going to retire so that I could finally marry you."

I dropped the phone, then I quickly recovered and pressed the phone back to my ear. "Hello?"

"You alright, major?"

"Yes. I mean—yes, I'm alright—but I was saying, yes, I will marry you."

He laughed. "Kiki, I hadn't asked the question yet."

"You basically did!" I nearly squealed.

"I actually thought you'd say no at first."

"I... I love you, Claudius."

Silence.

"I don't know why I said that," I quickly recanted.

"No, I'm in shock. I thought I was the only one in love. I've loved you since the day I met you. I can't do life without you again."

"Ask me then—ask me to marry you."

"Over the phone?"

"Come on, Ollie!"

"Alright," he chuckled. "Keoni Banks, will you make me the happiest man in the world and marry me?"

I smiled deeply, feeling the back of my head swell in pain from all the grinning. "Yes, Claudius, I will marry you."

14

I Will Go Up Against the Land Of Unwalled Villages

Zion

"Hey, Rein, you think you'll be chosen for one of the special forces teams?" Gabriel asked. He was shorter and thicker than me, but he kept up really well during all the physical exams. Thankfully, Gabriel was in the same platoon as me because we became battle buddies immediately.

"Honestly, I hope not," I said as I rolled my socks. We had one more day of testing, and then a day off before graduation, so I'd begun packing my things.

Three months seemed to breeze by once I got used to the tortuous training. The late nights and early mornings, paired with the physical work and mental work all day. I was left starving initially until I was able to stuff down the food they gave us in the five minutes we were allowed to eat during the first month. I also learned to eat whatever was in front of me, whether I liked it or not. But those were small things in the bigger picture.

"Come on, can't you see us?" Gabriel said as he laid back in bed. "Me, you, Carter, Grace, and Diaz; all of us as rangers or berets. That's the dream."

"You know, I clearly remember you hating the draft and being totally confused as to how anyone could dream of joining the military willfully when we first arrived."

He snorted and raised his hand towards the ceiling as if he was counting his five fingers. Gabriel was quiet for a moment, looking up at his hand above him. "I never thought I could do it. I never thought I'd make it."

Quietly, I continued to roll my Army issued green socks as Gabriel went on.

"When I was a kid, I was abused. When my grandparents finally took me in, they barely had enough for themselves, so I was just a burden. I ran away so many times, my grandparents stopped asking the police to look for me." A chuckle, weighed down with emotions, escaped him as he reflected. "I thought I'd never be anything more than a part-time employee, hopping from job to job. Now I'm a soldier. I have a purpose, and I'm not that stupid broken kid anymore. I made it out, and I never thought I would."

"That's why you want to join the special forces team? You want to go further."

"Yeah," he said with a small smile. His hand finally lowered, and he looked over at me. "What about you, Reinhardt?"

"I've told you already. I grew up in the church life until I got my girlfriend pregnant. That's kind of it. Nothing spectacular, except for the timing."

"I can't believe you've got a kid on the way. Does the little one make you work harder?"

"To be honest, I never thought about my daughter. I've only thought about Abigail, how much she's had to do alone."

"I see. You're worried about her?"

"Not exactly. I guess I missed her more than I thought I did."

Gabriel went on to explain his first crush to me, and how he still loved her, but I sank into my own thoughts. The day before I left for training, I slipped up and told Abbey that I loved her out of nervousness. I'd told her that before, and I didn't think I actually meant it this time, despite the passionate lovemaking we had that night. However, once I was away, Abbey was all I thought about. And every time we got a chance to call home, I called Abbey first, and then my parents.

I didn't think I've truly meant any word I said about love until now. Because every time I hung up the phone, I never forgot to tell her that I loved her.

"So, if you become an infantry man, I guess I'll fail the special forces test on purpose to join you."

"What?" I looked up from the socks to see Gabriel sitting up now.

"You're never listening to me." He rolled his eyes and hopped down from the top bunk.

"I'm sorry. You mentioned Abbey and I just started thinking about her."

"I can't wait until graduation to meet this girl."

"She won't be there," I said quickly.

"Why not?" A dark brow was raised as he lowered himself to his own bag to begin packing up. We had to be completely cleaned out before the graduation ceremony and no one else in our barracks had done any packing yet. Granted, we were all exhausted every day, so I understood. Besides, who'd come this far just to not pack and end up spending another three months here in misery because we didn't graduate?

"She's about to pop. I don't think the drive would be good for her," I lied. My parents still had no idea about Abigail who has been staying at a friend's house while I've been gone. I wanted her to stay at my place, but after my mother continued to come by to check on the apartment, Abbey left in fear that she'd be found.

"Oh yeah, she's eight months now, isn't she?" Gabriel asked.

"Somewhere around there."

"Am I at least invited to the Christening?"

"Of course, Gabby."

"Perfect," he said as he began rolling his own clothes.

— ÷ —

Tomorrow, graduation would take place, so tonight, I wanted to spend at least a few minutes alone in the chapel. Gabby was

150

going to hang out with some of our platoon guys, and I didn't want to go. I was about to go home, about to be fully immersed into the Christian culture again. I needed to say something to God. Anything at all, since He and I had grown distant. Or rather, I'd grown apart from Him.

Pulling open the chapel doors, I spotted a woman sitting on a bench. She was all alone in the small area. A large cross hung above the altar with a shimmering white stone platform. I'd only been to the chapel for service a few times, mostly because I was just too tired to go in the morning. But now, standing here looking at the cross ahead of me, I felt like this was my chance to get things right again.

"You coming in or what?"

I looked over at the woman as I stood in the doorway. I recognized her as a drill sergeant.

"Sorry, Drill Sergeant. I'll come back."

"No, no." She waved. "Come sit with me."

I nodded and found my way over to her. Banks had been an awfully kind drill sergeant compared to everyone else. Even when she made me do that stupid disassembling exercise like a thousand times, she had instructed me without demeaning me—unlike most of the other drill sergeants. Though I know they didn't mean any of it, and were just strengthening our mental fortitude, I still hated it, and I was looking forward to graduating just to get away from them.

"Drill—"

"Keoni," she corrected me without hesitation.

151

"Um—uh," I stammered, almost afraid to call her by her name. But she giggled, and it sounded like Abbey's girlish laugh.

"You can call me Major Banks if it makes you more comfortable."

I nodded, releasing a breath. "Major Banks, I didn't mean to interrupt you."

"You didn't. I was just thinking." She sighed as she looked away. Up close, and without a creased forehead from all the aggression, Major Banks looked kind, regal even. She had smooth brown skin and was youthful. Her shoulder length haircut made her look even younger without her large military hat.

"What do you think of Him?" she asked, catching me off guard.

"Who?"

"God."

"My thoughts on God?"

She nodded.

"Major Banks, I'm not—"

"Sorry," her gaze finally met mine, "I'm not supposed to ask about religious views. They say it infringes on privacy." She waved a hand like she didn't care.

"No, Major Banks, you're not infringing on my privacy. I just really wasn't sure how to answer your question."

Her brows lifted. "I see. It's an odd question to ask, but war makes even the strongest of us wonder if someone will protect us. Will we make it back this time? Is this the end?

Every day that question is asked by every soldier who steps foot onto the battlefield, and every day the answer gets a little foggier."

"You think God has the answers?"

"I don't know. I've always been told He does, but I have no idea if that's true."

"Have you ever asked Him?"

"Have you?"

"A few times." I shrugged as I turned to look at the cross. "Sometimes He answers right away, but most times He takes His time. So, it's not that God doesn't have the answers, we just don't wait for them." I smiled to myself as I caught a glimpse of Major Banks' shock. I was equally as shocked to find myself able to speak to someone about God the way my father does. Maybe I could get myself together after all. I felt hopeful again, which was exactly what I'd been missing; hope.

"Recently," I started in the silence, "like *really* recent, I realized I'd been missing hope. I did a study on the word before. In Hebrew, hope actually means *expectation*. But the Hebrew word comes from the root word that means rope or cord, or *to wait upon*."

"Hope?" She thought for a second and nodded for me to keep going.

"I had no expectations of God. I believed in Him because I was told to. But once I realized that I was missing hope, I realized I was missing faith too. Have you ever heard the scripture, *faith is the substance of things hoped for, the evidence of the things unseen?*"

153

"Once or twice when I was younger."

"Well, in that scripture, faith is described as the substance for hope. Which just means that faith is the insurance for what you're hoping for."

"What do you mean?"

"If hope is your expectation, then faith is the materialized matter in your hand." I held out my palm, recalling all the times my mother explained this scripture to me. "Your expectations are the locations on a map, but the car you drive in and the gas inside of the car is faith. Getting in the car is an act of faith, and divine expectation that you'll go where you intend. That's why faith is the substance, the ground that the root of expectation takes hold in."

She scoffed, but not indignantly, just in surprise. "That's a lot to take in."

"Sorry. I always get caught up with that scripture. It helped me to believe in God when I was younger. Mostly the second half of the scripture."

"The second half?"

"The part where the scriptures says that *faith is the evidence of things unseen*. It just means that faith, believing in God, having an expectation, is proof that God exists. He is unseen, but when you begin to hope for something, an opportunity for faith to develop rises, and with that, proof that God exists suddenly appears in your own life."

She was quiet for a moment, looking off as she thought in silence. "So, when I questioned if God had all the answers, there was already proof of His existence there, wasn't it?"

I smiled. "Yes! You believed in God, there is a seed of faith somewhere inside you. Because if you didn't believe, you would never question God, and since faith is proof that God exists, you ultimately have faith. Besides, you can't question what doesn't exist, can you?"

"Where did you come from?" She laughed. "Reinhardt, you're funny. If you know so much about God, and have studied Him, why aren't you a member of the clergy? Then you would've been exempt from all this."

"I..." I trailed off, unsure how to answer. "I know a lot about Him, but I don't practice what I preach."

I had never admitted that to anyone but myself. I've never even said it to Jala or Abbey, I just figured we all knew that we were wrong. We just didn't care. Or maybe I did care, but the pleasure outweighed the righteousness, and the flesh was not submissive to the Spirit. It wasn't the sex, it wasn't the women, it was the deception.

Sneaking around and doing things I wasn't supposed to breathed life into the sex. It made it more erotic, it put pleasure in an action that was pleasureless and empty when shared with anyone outside of marriage. But every time Jala, or Abbey, or any woman got into my bed, I felt like I had scored something. Like I had one-upped everyone because no one knew what I was doing. It became a point of pride. I was proud of my deception, and the sad part is that I never even considered it deceptive until now.

"But I beat my body into submission, in fear of preaching the Gospel to others, I myself am disqualified." Major Banks'

155

expression was soft as she shrugged. "That's my favorite verse of the Bible, the main one I remember, the one that helped me through the military. Yet, I don't follow it. And I don't even know why." She looked off, and her thoughts of her own sin were nearly palpable. "I'm sorry," Major Banks said finally, "I shouldn't have gone so far."

"No, this is good for me. I enjoy talking about God, I'm just struggling to do the right thing."

She sighed. "Sometimes, I feel like I'll never get there. Because what I want, and what God wants just don't match up. I know I should choose God's path, but I have everything I've ever wanted. I've got a boyfriend who cares about me, a lifestyle that's really good, and I've got a decorated military career, holding some of the most honorable positions in the Army and I'm only twenty-six. So, how do I choose?"

I jerked away and stared at her. Major Banks' demeanor was so settled and mature, I thought she was a young-looking older woman. Not someone close to my age.

"You're kidding, right?"

Her question faded for a moment and a proud smile captured her lips. "Not kidding at all. Your drill sergeant is twenty-six."

"That's incredible," I said with a little more amazement in my voice than I wanted. I was afraid I was going to offend her, but she raised a shoulder, still holding that smile.

"You know, my career is rare, but it's not that special."

"Why do you say that?"

"I've seen your paperwork, and your scores. If you'd joined the military at eighteen you could've been a very decorated solider by now. You're good, physically, and mentally."

I chuckled as I slumped in the pew. "I don't know. I prefer to lay low."

"I'd said the same thing, but you'd never believe I've been a guerrilla in the Green Berets, seen two tours, lost an eye, and became a drill sergeant. All while finishing college and moving through the ranks, just to land a spot as a major during unprecedented times."

"You lost an eye," I said mostly to myself.

"It's not as bad as it seems." She pulled her patch off. There was a scar tracing down from her brow to just past her lower lash line. And there was another scar across the side of her face beneath her eye.

"Can you open it?" I asked without thinking.

She laughed, unnerved by my crude question. "Do you really want to see a faded eye?"

"I-I've never seen one before."

She closed the other eye and took a breath. Slowly her eyes opened together, and just as she said, her brown right eye was faded to a nearly grey color.

"Completely blind in my right eye, and three percent of my hearing is gone in my right ear. All from one attack."

I was staring, *gawking* at her blind eye. She wasn't smiling, but she wasn't frowning either. Maybe the Major felt the eye patch was a badge of honor in itself, however, looking at yourself and facing reality that you're down to half your vision and a little of your hearing was missing probably wasn't easy. Realizing that you've given a part of you to a country that is still failing is hard to swallow. I didn't know if I was willing to give parts of me away the way the major had. But… learning that she'd stayed in the military even after she lost her eye made me believe that maybe there was something worth fighting for here.

"Well, Reinhardt, I better get going. You've got personal training before the ceremony. It's our last one together," she said as she pulled her patch back on.

"You're still beautiful, Major Banks."

She froze and turned to me quickly. I thought she'd snap at me, but she actually looked like she would cry. I probably shouldn't have said that. It was totally inappropriate. But it just kind of came out without giving me a chance to stop it.

Swallowing, she stood. I realized the major was in her civilian clothes. A cropped sweatshirt, and baggy sweats that were stuffed into her boots. I couldn't stop staring at her smooth skin exposed beneath her cropped shirt. My eyes drifted up to meet hers, and she smiled.

"We're the same age, Reinhardt, not the same rank, so you can't hit on me."

"Yes, Drill Sergeant. Sorry, Drill Sergeant." I looked away, but her laughter filled the entire church with a gentleness that eased the moment between us.

"Anyone special coming tomorrow?" She changed the subject.

"My parents."

"No girlfriend or wife?"

"My girlfriend is pregnant, but we haven't told my parents yet."

She nodded, and I realized how awkward I'd made things now. I've got a pregnant girlfriend, but I was completely mesmerized by my drill sergeant.

"Yikes," she said. "Hopefully they'll go easy on you then. Well, goodnight, Reinhardt." She waved as she inched through the pew to the exit.

"Keoni," I called her name for the first time, and she stopped immediately.

A raised brow and a small smile captured her plump lips. "Yes?"

"Thanks for not being a drill sergeant tonight. I really needed that."

Placing a hand on her hip, she leaned across the pew and extended the other to me. "When rank doesn't matter, I'd like to think we're friends."

I stood and clasped my hand in hers. "Me too, Major Banks.

— ÷ —

The graduation ceremony was shorter than expected. I said goodbye to Gabby who now made me call him *Private* Gabby, and a few more of my platoon before running into Major Banks and telling her bye too. And when I finally met up with

159

my parents, it was the most relief I'd had in a while. Despite how I got here, and how furious my parents were that President Fallon never once returned my father's calls, they were both proud of me.

Mom made me dinner. Smothered turkey legs, mustard greens, macaroni and cheese, cornbread, slow-cooked yams in a sweet syrup. I ate a really good meal. For most of the training, we were on rations. Not because we were in any kind of danger, but because it was part of our training. Possibly going to war meant that on the battlefield, for however long we're there, we won't get hot meals. There'll be days with no food, but we must survive.

Throughout dinner, I could hardly focus. I was so anxious to see Abbey, I couldn't wait. I'd made up my mind about her. After talking to Major Banks, I felt like I'd reconnected with God. I felt like, if nothing else, I really had a reason to come back to Him.

Being in training made me rethink a lot of things, and opening up finally about the things I've been doing in secret really helped me reconsider my life with Abigail. We're living together, we're having a child together, it only made sense to marry her. Marriage had never truly been off the table; I just hadn't been sure if I was ready for that kind of commitment.

It was silly. To be uncertain of committing to marriage just to continue to live with Abbey as if we're married was stupid. But, after being forced to be committed to the Army for three months, I began to think that maybe I can be committed to Abbey too.

As I approached my door, the nerves began to bubble over in anxiety. Gripping my bags, I knocked on the door and waited for a response. I'd texted Abbey and told her I'd be home today, but she didn't respond. With a sigh, I pulled out my keys and opened the door.

"Surprise! Welcome home, Zion!"

I gulped as I found Abbey, round, and very pregnant, standing in the middle of the foyer beneath a 'welcome home' banner. Balloons were all over the floor, confetti everywhere, and there were gift boxes wrapped in fatigue paper, stacked on the coffee table in the living room.

I slowly lowered my bags to the floor and looked around at everything. "Abigail, I can't believe you did all this."

"Do you like it?" She waddled over with a big smile.

"I love it." I pulled her into me for a hug, and her big bump crushed everything I'd just eaten in my belly, but I hugged her anyway. "Let's get married, Abbey," I whispered as we embraced. I'd missed her more than I thought I did when I realized I didn't want to let her go. It had only been three months, but it felt longer somehow.

"Ok," she whispered back. "Let's get married."

In the quiet of my place, I sank to my knees, still holding Abigail. I'd fallen in love with her, and she'd fallen in love with me too. Maybe things would finally be alright. Maybe, if I could fall in love and settle down, and even begin my journey back to God, then it was possible that the world wouldn't fall apart. It was possible that the times wouldn't be unprecedented for long. It could even mean that maybe the end of the world had—

My thoughts stopped when my phone rang. Abbey and I peeled apart. She wiped at her nose, face and body still gleaming with a radiance I wanted to be submerged in.

"Who is it?"

I squinted at my screen and scoffed. "It's my mom."

"Calling already?"

"She's probably just checking on me. Making sure I got home." I laughed as the phone hung up. I was putting it back into my pocket when it began ringing again. "It's my mom... again."

Abbey chewed her nail. "Pick it up, then."

I nodded. "Hello?" I answered as I placed the phone to my ear.

"Zion! It's happening!"

"What's happening? Mom, calm down, and speak clearly. What's going on?"

Abbey was squinting now, a worried look on her face as my mother sniffled into the phone.

"It's started, Zion. Russia just invaded Israel. The Gog Magog War has begun, and the world is about to end!"

So basically ... I was wrong about everything. My life really is over.

15

To Seize Spoil and Carry Off Plunder

Keoni

"Jensen?" I called as I stepped into the house.

I'd spent the rest of graduation day helping clean the barracks and get things prepped for the next recruits. That rookie, Zion Reinhardt, turned out to be a good guy. I enjoyed our conversation, I even thought about it on my drive home.

I'd gotten this sense of urgency when we talked that still hadn't left me two days later. It was like this was my chance, my *last* chance to get things right with God. For so long I had avoided Him, even in my thoughts, but now I wasn't so sure anymore.

My front door was unlocked, and only pushed up like Jensen had been in a rush when he'd come in and hadn't fully closed it. *Maybe he needed to rush to the bathroom,* I laughed to myself. Setting down my gear, I spotted shoes... *women's* shoes.

Any thoughts I had about God quickly vaporized as I picked up the strappy heels. I turned them in my hands, assuring myself that the shoes were not mine. I finally had a reason to leave Jensen, and it didn't sting in the slightest bit. I felt a little guilty, like I shouldn't try to find out who the shoes belonged to. I should just leave. I should take the chance I have to retreat and start over without Jensen… without Ollie.

I could just disappear… but that was impossible. I loved Ollie, and I wanted to be with him; so, in that moment, I decided to set things right with Jensen once and for all.

I crept through the house, quietly reaching the stairs—then I stopped. There was a shirt I recognized as Jensen's lying on the steps. Along with his khaki pants and socks that matched his shirt. From head to toe, the clothes that lay there were purchased by me, and he'd shed them for another woman. As if he was shedding me, his old skin, for her, a new skin. Whatever the case, Jensen couldn't wait to be out of his clothes, couldn't even wait to make it to the bedroom.

What if I hadn't been cheating on him? I thought as I walked up the stairs. *What if I'd been the loyal woman he assumed I was—how would I feel? Did the distance really cause this?*

Reaching the top of the steps, I could hear them in the bedroom. Jensen was a fool. Cheating on the person who'd been footing most of the bills and who provided you with a home. I guess it didn't really matter. The girl he's cheating with probably has a place he can crash at, *well, I hope she does for his sake.*

Tiptoeing down the hall, I looked at the walls lined with pictures of Jensen and me. We were happy once, genuinely happy. But then I began to miss Ollie, even when I wouldn't confess it to myself, and our relationship became a burden to me. I tried to love Jensen, but it was hard when the days were long, and Ollie wasn't there anymore.

I stopped at one picture; it was our third date at a fall festival. We were sporting milk mustaches from the frothy spiced lattes we'd been drinking, and we were smiling. Smiling like lovers as he held me close. I smiled a little, pressing a hand to the picture.

"I'm sorry, Jensen." I whispered.

Pulling the picture from the wall, I headed to our bedroom door and stopped. They were still going at it, so it didn't matter when I interrupted. Yet, I was suddenly feeling emotional. I wasn't sad that Jensen was cheating, I was sad that I had ruined something so perfect. From the pictures on the walls, Jensen and I looked like eternity would get tired of us. But that just wasn't the case anymore.

I took a deep breath and pushed open the door.

I stood there for a moment before Jensen looked over and saw me in the doorway. He tossed the girl to the side, and she yelped as she hit the bed. The two of them grabbed for blankets before the woman opted for a sheet as Jensen pulled the covers totally away from her in his frenzy.

"Keoni," he said, out of breath. "Sweetheart, it's not what it looks like."

I glanced around the room and found a dark blue uniform shirt with a badge attached to it. The shirt was small, so I figured it was the woman's, especially since Jensen's clothes were on the stairs and his underwear was wrapped up in the twisted sheets on the bed. I looked back at him; he was flushed with a slew of emotion riddling his face.

"I see why you joined the police force."

"I swear, that's not true. Please—" he stood up, but I took a step back.

"Most days I blamed myself," I said as I raised the picture to look at it again. "But now I don't know who to blame. Who's the real monster here? The one who stopped being happy, or the one who found happiness elsewhere? But how could I blame you? My job made me smile before I met you, and it'll make me smile again when you're gone."

If only Jensen knew that the real monster was the one who found happiness elsewhere, then he'd know I was the real jerk between us.

"Keoni, baby, listen to me. This was just a mistake. I'm sorry." He was panting as he spoke. Looking at Jensen now, I remembered why I'd been swooned by him. Broad shoulders, a gentle smile, and a kind demeanor. Jensen was a gentle giant that left you to discover his mysteries. It was entertaining for a while, keeping me busy from thinking of Olliare. However, mysteries can become longwinded when they aren't written well, and very unentertaining.

"I'll be gone for a while. I'm not sure when I'll return, but whenever I do, you need to be gone." I glanced over at the woman who was hiding behind Jensen. "Did you know this was my house? That those are my sheets?"

She swallowed, and that was answer enough. How couldn't she know? Our pictures lined the wall, and I'm certain this wasn't their first time here.

"If saving the nation doesn't keep his pants zipped, what makes you think saving a city will?"

I walked into the room and Jensen met me halfway.

"Keoni, will you just give me a minute to explain? I swear—"

I extended the photo to him, shoving it into his bare chest when he didn't take it. "Remember when we were happy? When did it change, Jensen? *Why* did it change?"

I had all the answers; what I was doing to him wasn't fair. His pathetic look, the swelling tears, Jensen was already remorseful.

"Keoni, please…"

I chewed my lip, glancing around the room before backing out. I never thought I'd see the day that Jensen Lyons cheated on me, but he did. And now I felt emotional because it was all my fault.

— ÷ —

I drove around the city into the night before I reached headquarters. I took the back entrance and stayed in Ollie's office all night looking over paperwork. There was so much I didn't know because my top-secret clearance was situational.

167

Being a drill sergeant didn't require any kind of clearance, so I didn't have it. And since Ollie and I barely spoke for three months, there was much for me to spend the night catching up on. Though, I'm certain my official duties would take a backseat as they always had once Ollie showed up tomorrow. Was it selfish to love without restraints?

I guess if you weren't a general and a major with top-secret clearance, strict duties to protect our nation while part of the world was at war, it wouldn't be selfish. But Ollie and I weren't civilians. The good of the USA was supposed to be our primary objective, but I was struggling to do the right thing. Just like I'd been struggling in my faith to do the right thing and prioritize God.

In the morning, around five, the door to Ollie's office opened, and he stepped inside whistling a tune. I wasn't surprised at his arrival; Ollie always came to work early. But he was surprised at *my* arrival. I'd told him I wouldn't be able to swing by the office until the evening in anticipation of spending time with Jensen, but plans changed, obviously.

Ollie stopped abruptly when he found me inside, sitting on his desk, turning pages in a folder.

"Kiki!"

"Good morning, Ollie." I gave him a little wave with a smile as he rushed over to me.

Lifting me off the desk, I gasped playfully before he kissed me. "I missed you so much," he said as he kissed me again. "When did you get here? I was expecting you later. I had a

168

whole setup I was going to do." He slowly lowered me back to the desk, where I began my pitiful confession.

"Well, I've been here since late last night, actually."

"In the office?" He frowned.

"Yes, sir."

"Why?"

Admitting to being cheated on was more embarrassing than actually being cheated on. "I walked in on Jensen and a woman from the police force."

He stepped back as if I'd just slapped him. "Are you okay?"

"I'm fine." I shrugged.

"Are you sure?"

"I'm positive." I reached for his shoulders.

Ollie looked disappointed and worried. And after a moment of silence, he shook his head, stepping forward so my hands could rush over his frame. "I'm going to kill him."

"Ollie, it's not a big deal. I needed an excuse to break up with him anyway. This worked out for us."

"He can't do that and get away with it."

"Earth to Ollie." I snapped my fingers beside his ear. "I've been cheating on him too. It's not a big deal. I'm fine, I promise."

He sighed, pulling me closer to the edge of the desk. "Are you sure you don't need me to make you feel better?"

I blushed. "I'm not sure at all, General Saint Olliare."

He grinned as he leaned down and kissed me. "I'm glad you're finally mine now."

"Has my heart ever belonged to anyone else?"

We both laughed until Ollie began to look distant. I noticed he was looking at a folder stamped with the word **Israel** on the top. It was like the folder had triggered a bad memory.

"Ollie? What's wrong?"

He took a step back, leaving me on the desk to circle the room. "Have you heard the news?" he asked.

"What news?"

"That Russia invaded Israel, and on the same day, China retreated from the brawl they were having with us on the waters."

"What?" I hopped from the desk and came over to him. "I read through paperwork last night, there wasn't a single memo about either of these things."

"That's because this happened just last night. The memos were sent via email, nothing printed. We held a virtual meeting with the Secretary of Defense and the President in the middle of the night last night."

"What is going on?" I asked as I flopped onto the couch. Ollie had already mentioned that things had turned south when China and the US began a naval war. The Chinese forces were fighting with speedboats, almost like modern day pirates attacking cruise ships. They were launching missiles into pressure points on our ships because they knew them inside and out.

China had at least a fleet of fifty American ships that was a collection of working ships from the countries they'd invaded. They knew our craftsmanship, and even though we'd made improvements, they were minor in comparison.

"That's not even the worst of it," Ollie said as he sat beside me. "The submarines that were supposed to be used on the sank ships were either intercepted by Chinese forces, or when the ships sank, removed somehow underwater."

"What are you saying?"

"I'm saying that from the now six sank ships, when divers went to recover what they could, the submarines were missing. Soldiers are missing. Submarines that'd made contact with our communications went off grid and have not been found."

"So, you think Chinese forces took those too? That's impossible."

"Not if they planned for it," he said with deep sigh.

"What does the president think?"

"What everyone else thinks. China's been planning for this, and the five years of peace was just a really good hand dealt to them. It worked in their favor."

I shook my head. "But what did he say about them retreating?"

He tossed his hands up in frustration. "We don't know why they retreated. Reports came in during our meeting that there were no more Chinese soldiers in Taiwan. There were Indian and Nepali soldiers in Chinese uniforms to continue the invasion."

"There are no Chinese soldiers? Have we located them?"

"We're on that now. We've got drones flying the entirety of Taiwan to see if they retreated to some hideout."

I leaned back, covering my face in exhaustion already. "Clearly, China and Russia are working together. Are our forces checking the Russia-Ukraine territory?"

"It's been cleared. Just Russian forces."

"Why would China retreat the same hour Russia invaded Israel?"

"Like you said, they're working together."

"But why?"

He scratched his head, staring ahead at his blank wall across from us. "All we know is that Israel is a goldmine. You invade them and take over; you've got enough supplies to put your economy on top. China knows this. Russia knows this."

"So you think they're splitting the goods."

"It's the only explanation."

Sitting for a moment, I thought over what I knew so far. With Russia and China launching attacks on sweet spots for the US, it seemed less likely that Israel had been the target all along.

"What if Israel is just a bonus, and Taiwan is just a starting point?"

Ollie looked over at me, but he didn't speak.

"What if all this was just so that China could conquer the US?"

"You seriously think we haven't considered that?"

"No, because if it had been considered, plans for a full war would be in place. Not small mitigations."

"We always plan for the worst, you know that."

"Do we? Or do we plan for the *planned* worst? What if those submarines arrive in US waters—what will we do?"

Ollie adjusted, annoyed that I wasn't letting this go. Ollie had more say than I did in the meetings, but there was only so much he could suggest. Of course, there'd been discussion of China's planning, however, we've been avoiding one topic when it comes to war; where will the battle be fought?

American cities haven't been touched by war since the Civil War. We've sent troops to countries all over to help them win but fighting on our own turf hadn't been considered. And truly, it felt like no one wanted to consider that China might bring the war to us.

"This was a lot to come back to," Ollie said as he grabbed my hand and changed the subject. "But I'm glad you're here. Kiki."

"Me too," I said.

I decided to let the topic go, let all the questions sink to the back of my head for now. My leaders were capable men and women, and I couldn't let myself be worried. I had to trust them.

Trust that they would plan for the very worst, even if they didn't want to. I didn't need to convince them, and I didn't need them to convince me we would be ready because, deep down, we all knew what China's silence meant. They fooled us once with their kindness, but it'll be a day of reckoning for the US if we let their silence fool us now.

173

16

Prophesy Against Him

Claudius

A meeting was called once everyone arrived at headquarters. We all had been moved up a rank since Collins was named General of the Army and moved to Washington three weeks ago.

I got that promotion I wanted, I was officially a Major General, sporting two stars. Keoni flipped when she finally noticed them. But she flipped once more when I pinned her with a silver oak leaf, naming her Lieutenant Colonel. Since she was on this team, we all got promoted. Even Captain Luther finally made Major, though I voted to keep him at the rank of captain. Nonetheless, Keoni, who was all mine now, was finally a colonel, and it took her a fraction of the time to get there.

"What are we going to do about Russia invading Israel?" Lieutenant General Jacobs asked before the meeting could start. We were all seated, but there was an order we usually followed. I guess not today though, since the now four star general, Samus Murphy, gave him a reply that set the tone for a wildfire of a meeting.

"What do you think we should do, Jacobs?"

"*Something*, while we've got the chance. China is retreating. We can regroup our own forces and help Israel at the same time."

"I agree." Whitney nodded. She was a full bird colonel now, with more to offer and more weight to her words.

"You agree that we should recoup and split our forces to help Israel?" Murphy asked.

"I do, sir. I think that if we lend a hand to Israel, they can lend a hand to us. Resources, food, anything we might need right now."

"I think she has a point," I said.

Whitney glanced back at me, and I gave her a wink. It made her blush, but it made my new lieutenant colonel's back straighten as Banks caught the exchange between us. It didn't mean anything, and I only supported Whitney because she'd been supportive of me in meetings while Keoni had been gone. We'd kept it professional for the most part. There was a little flirting here and there, she even stayed late one night in my office. I was tempted, very tempted, but I sent her home with a peck on the cheek and my gratitude for her hard work and dedication.

"Would you explain further?" Murphy insisted.

"It doesn't need further explanation." I nodded as I sat back in my seat. "We help Israel, they help us. They're one of the only countries around that doesn't have some sick and twisted tie back to China, preventing them from aiding us."

"And we've got nothing to offer anyone," Vice Admiral Zhao added. He spoke up quite often in our meetings with the joint forces. The Navy and the Marines had been heavily involved in our meetings. And, as of last night, the Air Force has stepped up to provide more air support for special forces missions to sniff out the Chinese hiding spot if it's not in Taiwan.

"So, basically, we're broke and we need help to win this war, and it still makes sense to split our forces to everyone?" Murphy deadpanned.

"If I can speak candidly," a marine general equivalent in rank to Murphy joined the discussion. "We wouldn't be in this position if we'd made a decision about rescuing those soldiers sooner. We took too long, and let our men get desperate."

"They rushed in without a plan, and broke protocol thinking they'd be heroes," Hunter said harshly. He was sitting toward the front of the table, eyeing every one of us as he spoke. "It's no one's fault that those soldiers rushed in without clearance. We just need to come up with a solution."

"There is no solution," Admiral Zhao nearly snapped. "We've got China retreating, Russia invading Israel, and our men are still fighting for Taiwan. The only thing we can do is retreat from Taiwan."

"You know the Secretary of Defense won't go for that."

"Then he has sentenced this country to her death!" The Admiral stood abruptly and rushed from the room.

We all watched him exit in anger and frustration. We were all passionate, that's why we were here. That's why we've been fighting so hard and making tough decisions that no one else wanted to make because we love this country. We love our people.

"Let me talk to him," I said as I stood. "I know he's your guy," I said to the other admiral sitting at the table. He was as confused as the rest of us. "But I kind of know Zhao pretty well. His family is in shambles, so this is all very personal for him."

"He shouldn't be on the team then, because it's personal for all of us," Murphy said callously.

"I'm sorry, sir, I don't mean to put one's emotions over the other. Can you give me a chance to speak with him?"

Murphy sighed, flicking his wrist to send me away.

I nodded. "Thank you, sir. In my absence, please allow Lieutenant Colonel Banks to speak in my stead."

She looked up at me, and when I winked at her, she turned away, unamused. That stung when she didn't gush for me, however, it probably stung more for her since I'd just done the same thing to Whitney.

I decided not to even give Whitney a sideways glance. Instead, I headed out of the room in search of Zhao.

I found the admiral sitting in his office, with only one lamp on. I knocked on his door, though it was open.

"What do you want?" he said quietly. "I'm not apologizing."

"No need." I closed the door. "I simply came to check on you. I know this has been tough on you with part of your family in China. You may feel crossed."

"I don't," he said coldly.

Taking a breath, I tried not to let his comment bother me. "Well, then, maybe you're just tired, admiral. I don't know what's going on with you. You've been leaving work early, hard to get in contact with. What's up with you?"

"Nothing." He looked away.

"Come on, Ping," I used his first name, "what's up with you, man? Brother to brother."

"I am not your brother," he sounded like he was a scorned man. Torn and broken over the chaos in his heart. Fighting his homeland to protect the people of the country where he now resided.

"No, we're not brothers by parents, but we are by blood. The same sweat and tears and blood you've bled, I've shared in that too. Joining the military, we took an oath to be brothers, to become family. So, we may not share the same parents, Ping, but we share the same source, the same red, white, and blue blood pumping through our veins."

The vice admiral looked stunned, like in all his years of serving, no one had ever told him anything like what I'd said.

"You really want to know the truth?"

"Yeah," I said as I sat in a chair across from him. But he stood, moving to his window to peer out at the soldiers running PT on the track.

"Do you remember what I said before I left the meeting?"

"That the Secretary of Defense sentenced us to death if we don't pull out of Taiwan? Yeah, it was a little scary and disheartening."

"But it is the truth."

"What do you mean?"

He turned to me, moon shaped eyes void of all emotions. He opened his jacket and lifted the greenish tan shirt beneath it. There was a tattoo along his abdomen of a snake or maybe a wingless dragon, standing on its hind legs. He turned, and I could see the slithering body of the creature wrapping along his entire frame until it reached just below his collar bone, up the center of his chest. The mouth of the red creature was open and there were flames decorating the skin of his shoulders, painting all the way around to his back.

"I am a Red Dragon. Born and raised for this time. My mission was to reach America and become the highest-ranking officer I could become in the Navy before my time was called."

My eyes skirted up his frame until they met his. "What are you saying, Ping?"

"I'm saying that America's reign is over. Her stubbornness and pride will be her downfall."

"I don't think I understand." I sat forward very slowly. "Why are you telling me this? What am I supposed to make of this? *You*, a lifelong sleeper cell? Come on, Ping." I nearly laughed but his dead eyes stirred fear within me. "There's no way. This isn't you." I exploded to my feet. "This isn't you!"

"Keep your voice down, or you will never leave this office."

"Did you just threaten me?" I snapped.

He pulled his gun from his waist and raised it at me. "You have been very good to me, Claudius, and for that, I will not let you get caught up in all of this. Take the ones you love and get out of here before the week is out."

I stumbled back, bracing myself against the wall. "That soon? What's going to happen?"

"China is going to invade the US. The Red Dragon will storm the capital, and we will storm this headquarters. There are enough of us in this building to take this place down. We are already here, general."

"Ping, you know I have to tell someone. I can't let this happen."

"I am doing you a favor. But if you betray me, I will have that woman killed. The one you've been sleeping with in your office."

I stiffened. I could feel my shirt sticking to my back from nervous sweat, and I almost fell into a dizzy spell at the mention of Keoni.

"What... W-What are you talking about?"

"The new lieutenant, the one who'd been gone for three months training soldiers. You've been sleeping with her. And you two have been in a relationship for nearly her entire career."

"How did you know?"

"We are always watching. Watching everything and everyone. Determining who we can trust and who we cannot."

"No," I whispered as I looked blankly at his desk. There were papers all over it, I doubt he'd even cared to read any of them. I know I hadn't cared to read anything once Keoni and I began sharing an office again. Since our reunion, we've slacked in our work. Even with the world tipping off its axis, all I'd been focused on was Keoni. Now, her life was in danger, but so were the lives of millions, how could I choose?

I snapped my head up. "How can I choose? You think because you're pointing a gun at me and threatening me, that you can trust me? You think I'm going to make a choice between Keoni and my country? Because you say so?" I shook my head. "No. No! Let me tell you something, Ping, that's not how we do things here in the US."

"I know," he said softly as he lowered the gun. "You do things without remorse, without dignity. You all do things because you can, but never consider the outcome of all your senseless actions." He stepped closer. "You were not chosen because you could be trusted as a friend, general. You were chosen because you have much to lose."

I dropped my head, staring at my boots in silence. "You chose me because you trusted that I would react the way you believed I would. That I would value Keoni more than your betrayal. And what happens if I don't?"

"That won't happen. I can assure you that things are in place to keep your mouth sealed."

"Why, Ping?" I nearly choked on a sob. "Why are you doing this?"

"My homeland needs me. It has been a long-awaited desire of our people to rule the nations. But for decades, America stood in our way. And for decades, we plotted for her spiraling downfall. I didn't know if I'd live to see this day, and I am honored that I have been called. Finally."

"How could you?" I sniffled loudly as the tears began to fall.

"Because I was not raised to cry over betrayal, I was raised to expect it. To embrace it, to become the betrayer of the brethren."

I gritted my teeth as I leaned forward and covered my face. I had a choice to make. I could try to do something and save our nation. Or I could save Keoni. I loved Keoni with everything in me, and nothing in this world could amount to her place in my life. How could I risk her life? But how could I risk the lives of innocent people?

If I choose to act on the information I've gotten, I'll save the nation. But Keoni will die as a result. If I snitch on Ping, the Red Dragon will retaliate by killing her. But I'm a soldier. A soldier with information on an impending invasion. I can't ignore this intel.

But…

Will the country be worth saving if Keoni isn't there by my side when it's all over? Will she and I even survive the invasion? Choosing Keoni would mean the entire nation would be flooded with the rage of war.

The purpose of the US military was to protect civilians and our home from the threats of the world. When you join the military, when you climb the ranks, you forsake everything for the country. I've believed in the US my entire career, until Keoni stormed back into my life. I've become obsessed, totally absorbed by her beauty, and now, the country will pay for it.

Standing there, simply contemplating the survival of the nation made me a traitor. In my heart, I had already chosen Keoni, and I never gave America a fair chance. I didn't want to be a hero like I did when I was a kid. I just wanted to save Keoni, but that meant losing everything else.

I'm sure that was the point of all this. Forcing me to choose the nation meant losing Keoni who meant everything to me. Choosing Keoni meant I'd lose everything else. The Red Dragon had made their decision, and I had to make mine. Yet, I still faltered. What was the right thing to do?

The right thing didn't matter anymore. Stuttering over a decision like this had already made me a betrayer, no different than the sleeper cells who waited with deadly smiles. They were like the beauty of the Arctics. The frozen waters, the sparkling snow, it all drew you in and made you desire your own winter wonderland. However, even as the sun shined on the snow, the cold sapped all the heat from the atmosphere. It was like looking at pictures of space and never realizing there was no light, no heat, no oxygen in space.

How do you survive off of pretty pictures and dazzling images?

You don't.

"What am I supposed to tell everyone waiting at the meeting?" I asked as I wiped at my tears.

"Tell them I'm feeling better but I don't want to return to the meeting. I need a moment to myself."

"You really won't send an apology?"

"I owe this country nothing."

"But what about us? Your battle buddies? The ones you've fought with?"

"Daily, I have fought alongside the Red Dragon in hiding. We have—"

"Screw the Red Dragon!" I slammed my hands on his desk, panting in anger. I was sick of his calm demeanor, his superiority act. Of course, he sat on top of the world when, for decades, he'd carved out his own seat and planned the demise of it behind everyone's back.

"China isn't as strong as you think," I said as I recomposed myself. "We will fight back, and you will not take this country."

"We are ready, no matter how long it takes."

"Then your mind is made up?"

"Yes. It cannot be changed."

"A week," I whispered. "That's all I have."

"Don't do anything stupid and make me regret telling you the truth. I will make sure you are the last American to die if you interfere in any way."

Wiping a hand through my hair, I only found it in me to nod. The brokenness I felt inside was almost unbearable.

"You should return to your meeting now," Ping suggested.

Without another word, I turned for the door.

"One more thing, Claudius. If I knew, long ago, that there were truly good people in the western world, I think I might've reconsidered becoming a Red Dragon."

I looked over my shoulder. "I don't care."

With a grunt, I tanked open his door and stepped into the busy hall. Soldiers in different uniforms from each branch walked by. Everyone was preparing for the battle we knew was coming, we just didn't know when and where. I could shout right now, that the war was coming to us, but by the time I made it to the meeting room, I'm sure Keoni would be dead.

Slowly, my feet carried me back to the boardroom as I thought over the incident from a month ago.

Last month, for a week straight, the security system in the headquarters stopped working. It would go off randomly, making everyone spring into action. We were ready for an invasion then. But we aren't any longer, and it's all part of Ping's plan. He was the one who checked the systems for us initially. With a degree in computer science, he'd said he might know a thing or two on how to fix it until the maintenance guy could come out.

But after two or three days, we were used to the security system going off and no one paid it any attention. Even two weeks later, it went off again, and we hardly reacted, and last week, we laughed about it. We made jokes that the US Military couldn't afford a good security system. We joked that the maintenance team was getting paid for nothing. However, I now know the truth. We were being desensitized. Slowly, but surely, so when the alarms go off again, we'd never expect an invasion.

I stood at the boardroom door and took a breath. When I opened it, the first pair of eyes I locked with were Keoni's. She had a tired and annoyed expression on her face. She was so beautiful, so radiant. I had to protect her. I couldn't let her fall with the rest of this place. But that decision almost made me break into a screaming fit right in front of everyone.

I had chosen the love of my life over an entire country, a country I'd sworn to protect. But now, she was all I could focus on.

"Major General, would you like to take a seat?" Murphy asked as I stood there staring at Keoni.

"Sorry, general." I nodded as I stepped inside to find my seat. I forced a sarcastic grin to my face and said, "At least he apologized."

"To us? I didn't hear it." Murphy said.

"You wouldn't want to." I adjusted in my seat and let Murphy chew me out for my sarcasm. But I didn't miss the way Keoni looked me over. The way her concern became less professional by the second.

17

Put Hooks in Your Jaws

Keoni

After the meeting, Ollie and I spent most of the day apart. When we were together, we were in a group. There was so much to plan, so much to go over within our personal groups and teams, I struggled to stay focused. But when the day finally ended and we were off the clock, I found myself dragging down the hall to Ollie's office to retrieve my things.

"Colonel," he said quickly as I entered our shared office. It was as if he had been waiting for me. I passed him a glance as I relished the sound of him using my new rank. Being a silver leaf was still so fresh to me, but it sounded perfect whenever anyone used it.

"Yes, future husband," I said playfully as I crossed the room to my things.

He looked a little scruffy, like he was nervous or tired. But we were all nervous and tired. He smiled, and something felt off. But his smooth voice rolled out like silk as he playfully replied, "Future husband? I kind of like the way that sounds. But, plain ol' 'husband,'" his voice rang out over the thumping of his boots as he came over to me. Wrapping his arms around my waist, he whispered against my neck, "That'll sound even better once we're married."

As I turned in his arms, I caught a glance of a figure in the doorway.

"Ollie," I pushed him away, and he stumbled back with raised brows.

"Sweetheart, what's—"

"Admiral Zhao, we missed you at the rest of the meeting," I said quickly.

Ollie's eyes widened before he whipped around to face the vice admiral. "What are you doing here?" Ollie barked.

"Major General, Lieutenant Colonel, I was on my way out, and just stopped by to say goodnight. And to tell you, general, that things are looking up for me. Very soon, sooner than I initially thought, things will work out." He glanced over Ollie's shoulder to see me, but the general shifted, blocking me from Zhao's view.

What is going on? I thought as I watched the two men fight a silent battle before Zhao surrendered a smile.

"General, I expect you'll be good. You won't need anything from me."

"No," Ollie said dryly.

"Very, *very* good," Zhao said. "Well then, goodnight, general." He stepped to the side to find me behind Ollie. "And goodnight to the lovely colonel."

It seemed like his footsteps went on for an eternity before they eventually faded. Ollie lunged for the door and nearly slammed it closed.

"I know that door was closed, Ollie, he must've opened it," I said as he brushed by me. "Ollie, I'm sorry."

"Get your things," he said curtly. "We need to leave, now."

"Why?"

"Just..." Ollie sighed as he turned to face me; he looked unsettled, like the stress of one conversation had totally unraveled him. "I'm not mad at you at all. But I want us to leave now. I want you to come to my place tonight since you can't go to your home."

"What's going on?"

"And don't worry," he ignored me as he turned back to his bags, "I'll tell Hunter something and he'll let it pass that we're spending a few nights together."

"Wait, you're going to tell someone about us?"

"Just Hunter. He kind of already suspects it. So, I'll tell him you were so afraid that you ended up staying over or something."

"Ollie!" His name was like a gunshot going off in the office. It brought him to a jarring halt as he stood perfectly still, clutching his bag. "What is going on?" I asked in the silence. My voice was calmer now as I stared at his anxious frame.

"What was that just now with Zhao? Why are you hiding things from me?"

"Lieutenant," Ollie turned to me, a dry expression on his face. "Get your things. We are leaving and that's an order."

I stammered for a moment, trying to find the joke in his sudden change in behavior, but when his eyes were empty and his lips sagged into a frown, I knew something serious was happening. Too serious to talk here.

"Yes, sir," I finally said.

— ÷ —

I put the car in park once I pulled into my driveway. Ollie hadn't said a word to me since we left headquarters. After he returned from the meeting, he hadn't been himself. I tried to ignore it and he did too. But the tension between Admiral Zhao and the general was too high. It pulled his forced calm behavior into focus and made it suffocatingly obvious that whatever Ollie was hiding had something to do with the vice admiral.

I sat in my car as I waited for Ollie to pull up. He followed me home at a safe distance so I could park my car somewhere. Jensen's car was parked in the driveway. I wondered if he was alone, if he was packing his things, but I decided not to care. I needed to have a clear conscience for whatever Ollie was going to tell me tonight.

When his car finally pulled up, I got out of mine and into his. We didn't speak when we pulled off initially. The silence was aching, but I wouldn't talk. I was afraid that my voice in the deathly silence would make him snap. Obviously, whatever was going on was something Ollie had trouble putting into words.

When we were a few blocks from my house, he slowed to a red light and asked, "If someone placed a gun to your head and told you to either save the world or the one person you love, what would you do?"

I turned in my seat to look at him. The curtain of dark lashes around his eyes closed and opened slowly as he took a deep breath. The red hue from the traffic light on the empty dark street reached into our car, making the moment seem more intense than it already was.

"Ollie, what's—"

"It's an *extremely* hypothetical question. I just want to know what you'd do."

Exhaling, I looked ahead as the car pulled off from the light.

"Do you remember that night we spent driving around to every fast-food joint we could find with a working ice cream machine?"

He chuckled. "I do, but I don't know what that has to do with the question."

"Why is that day so memorable to you?"

He shrugged, raising a few fingers off the steering wheel. "I mostly remember you whining. But that night we spent nearly the whole night together in a car. We'd already driven fourteen hours to New York for the weekend and then you decided you wanted ice cream."

I smiled a little as I recalled the warm long weekend from a few years back. That was before Jensen when things were simple and sweet between Ollie and me.

"That was the day I fell in love with you."

He jerked to a halt at the stop sign and snapped his vision towards me. With his full attention, I said it again, "That was the day I fell in love with you, Ollie. I had never been in love before, had never been loved by anyone else. But you opened a new door in my life and took me by the hand through it to explore it with me. The world could not do that for me. Jensen couldn't do that for me. But you did." I paused as he began driving again. "Love... I wouldn't give that up for anything. The world is strong enough to start over again, but I'm not. Love is fragile and complicated, and finding someone to experience that with for the long run has an immeasurable impact on your life. A whole new person awakens inside because of love. So, I wouldn't save the world, I'd save the one who I'd start the world over with."

Silence ticked by as quickly as the streetlights. I didn't have much else to say because that was truly how I felt. There was so much more to consider, so many other factors that I ignored regularly for the sake of this relationship. But it was all worth it to me. I knew it was wrong to focus only on Ollie. I knew it was selfish to negate my duties most days just to laugh with my crush, to pass off work so Ollie and I got more time together. Yet, I couldn't stop myself. I allowed myself to be consumed because it felt good. I thought I loved my career, but, with the world in such a fragile state, I wanted to hold on to the one thing that would last me an eternity, and that was love. That was loving Ollie, despite how backwards it all was.

"I want you to know that I'm going to do everything I can to save you, Keoni." He reached for my hand and laced his fingers with mine as he pecked the top of it.

"Ollie, what's going on?"

"I can't tell you right now, but I will soon. Just trust me, promise me you'll trust me? And promise me that you know me, the real me. You know I love this country and I love you, and I would give my dying breath to protect both."

"Claudius, you're scaring me."

"Don't be scared," he said as he pulled into the driveway of a small log cabin. I hadn't noticed when we went off road a few blocks back.

"What am I supposed to make of this?"

"Of what?" Ollie looked down at me after parking the car. "Of the log cabin? It's pretty nice on the inside. I built it myself for when I needed to get away from everything."

"No, Claudius, you know what I mean."

He sat back and squeezed my hand. "Right now, the less you know the better."

"Alright then," I pulled my seatbelt off and adjusted to see him better. "I can promise you that I know you, and I know your intentions. And I promise to trust you. But you have to promise that you won't keep things from me forever. That at some point, you will tell me the truth."

He looked relieved as he leaned over to grab my other hand. "I promise I will tell you everything when I can. But for right now, I need to keep you in the dark for your security."

I nodded, though I was more nervous than ever. I could've vomited from nerves, but I had been a Green Beret for a year. Knowing there was highly classified information I wasn't privy to when I was a young soldier had never scared me, it used to excite me. It always meant there was more to come, more ways to use my skillset. However, when it came to Ollie, and his fear, highly classified information could break me.

The next morning, I could hear Ollie on the phone in the bathroom of the cozy log house. He was talking to Hunter, one of his friends and superiors. Immediately, I climbed from the wooden bed and found a uniform to slip into. Ollie and I had spent the night reminiscing about the past before drifting off to sleep. It was one of the most romantic nights we've had in a while.

When Ollie emerged from the bathroom, he was shocked to find me dressed and tying my boots up.

"You're not going," he said finally.

"I'm going to work." I pushed by him into the bathroom, but he stopped me.

"You promised to trust me."

"But I never promised to leave you to fight this battle alone. I'll fight blindly, but I'm not going to let you do whatever this is by yourself."

"Keoni—"

"I'll be ready in five minutes."

At headquarters, we were greeted at the door by General Murphy and Hunter. The two nodded at Ollie and did everything they could not to give him sideways glances as I followed him inside. We'd arrived together, in the same vehicle, everyone knew something was up. Had things been normal, we would've been questioned. Instead, Ollie and I were escorted upstairs in silence to an interrogation room.

As the doors opened, Ollie grabbed me by the arm and stopped me while the others filed in. Glancing over his shoulder, his eyes flicked back to mine in a controlled panic. It was a panic every soldier knew. The fear of the unknown. Fear that you've prepared for battle, yet there was no amount of preparation for the rage of war. Every soldier knew how to control their panic, because it was the fear that we lived for. The exhilarating fear that was our driving force to survive. Our fear was our strength.

"Listen, if things get crazy in there, I want you to run away as far as you can. Get to safety. Get back to the log cabin. If I'm not there, you run until you're far away from here. Run until you make it to Washington and get help."

195

He pressed a folded piece of paper into my hand. "Read that if things go crazy."

"Ollie, please—"

"Lieutenant," his voice was stern, snapping me back to focus. "That is an order."

I nodded, pushing away the nerves. "Yes, sir."

There was more I wanted to say, to ask, and I knew there was more Ollie wanted to say as well. But he did an about-face and headed into the room without another word.

I stepped into the control area after tucking away the letter. It was connected to the padded interrogation room. There was a haggard old woman with a round face and moon eyes looking around. She looked lost, like she wasn't sure where she was or how she got there.

I was just as lost as she was as I peered into the interrogation room. It was hardly used, padded with high tech foam to hide all the technology we used during an interrogation. Brain waves were monitored, heartbeats, even sentences were translated if spoken in another language. Trigger words were detected by our system, they were checked against the database to match anything in current events that might be linked.

"It's an interrogation," Hunter said. "You're only here at Olliare's request, so keep quiet." He nudged me before crossing the room to Ollie who was getting an earpiece placed into his ear, and a second recording device tucked into the pocket of his uniform.

I saw Hunter and Murphy exchanging words with Ollie, before he glanced over at me. He was worried, fearful. I swallowed, raising my chin at the general, and he nodded at me before opening the door and stepping inside.

"Who is this woman, sir?" I asked Hunter as he stood beside me.

"She showed up this morning, and said she had information that only Olliare would understand. Said she wouldn't talk to another soul."

I shifted, as I stood against the back wall of the room. I was a guest, invited to the interrogation at Olliare's request. Last night I promised to trust him, but now, I was afraid of that promise. I'd blindly allowed myself to trust him, but what reason did I have not to? Maybe I should've forced him to tell me what was going on, pried a little more. I wasn't sure. But it was too late now. Clenching my fists, I took a stilling breath as I watched and listened.

"Good morning, miss…?"

"I am Wang Mei," the old woman's voice was as grating as she looked.

"Wang Mei." Ollie nodded. "Is your first name Mei, then?"

"Yes."

"Well, Miss Mei, I'm Major General Claudius Saint-Olliare. I was told you were looking for me. You have specific information that only I would know, is that right?"

The woman nodded.

"And what does this information regard?"

"A war."

197

Hunter looked over at the woman set up at the desk in the corner. She was busy reading the heart monitor.

"There's been no change, sir," she said without looking away.

"That means she's not lying," he whispered to me.

I looked at the heart monitor for Mei's charts and then Ollie's. His heartbeat was only a little abnormal, nothing to worry about, but Mei's was completely normal as noted.

"A war? What war?"

"Why don't I tell you the story of the Red Dragon."

Ollie adjusted in his seat, giving her a nod to continue.

"Long ago, there was a serpent who slithered along the earth, sleek and quiet. His scaly body was strong and resilient, and he became a serpent to be feared. On those which he preyed, he left no remains. Yet, the serpent was not satisfied."

Mei leaned forward, like she was about to get to the interesting part of the story. A wrinkled hand stretched across the smooth wooden table as she said, "He'd eaten many things. Had gained much strength from everything he ate. From the scorpions, he gained venom. From the tarantulas, he gained legs. From the rats, he gained speed, and from the bombardier beetles, he gained their fire. However, the serpent knew he was missing something."

"What was he missing?"

"Wings."

Ollie folded his arms across his chest, watching her closely as she continued.

198

"The gain of wings would mean freedom, and it would mean he would be an unstoppable force. He would go wherever he wanted. He would be respected. And he would be revered."

The tall tale Mei was telling had begun to make me anxious. Shifting my weight from one foot to the other, I glanced around the room to see General Murphy. He was nervous as he stood by the door, watching through the one-way window. With Mei's vitals being void of any irregularities, her story made the general—the entire *room*—nervous.

Or maybe it wasn't her story. Maybe it was just the message of her tale, the true meaning behind it that frightened us. Since we hadn't gotten to that point, nerves ate away at each of us.

"Did he ever gain his wings?" Ollie asked.

"He did not," the woman answered in her old, raspy voice. "After many attempts, eating small birds and bats, even trying to eat fish to gain their fins, he came up short. And a new predator was on the horizon. One that was mighty, strong, swift. It was the only beast standing in the serpent's way, and he would prove that he was still the one to be feared."

"The serpent wanted to be feared. Why?"

"Fear is the only way to be truly respected."

"And you believe that?"

"I do." She glanced off, looking around. I wasn't sure what she could be looking at since the room was just padded with dark foam and a big one-way glass window and a smaller one on the door. "The serpent finally came face to face with the beast and was delighted for battle. He thought that he would finally earn his wings. However, the serpent was critically wounded during the fight, forever staining himself with his own blood. Turning his thick black scales and growing feathers a red color."

"He retreated after the beast wounded him, right?"

"Yes. He retreated, but he did not give up. The serpent ordered those who would normally be his prey to work for him and take down the beast, and in return, their lives would be spared."

"Alright." Ollie nodded as if he was actually interested in this story.

I felt my own nerves ready to boil over as we waited for this dragging story to end.

"In ordering his prey to fight for him, the serpent found that he would no longer be regarded as the one who slithers, but as the one who flies. The one who slithered had been defeated, but the one who would fly would never fall again. Thus, he named himself, the Red Dragon."

"So, he's technically still a serpent, but he's calling himself a dragon?"

"Not for much longer."

It was like a sweltering heat zipped through the room, gluing us to the walls and floors of the control room.

"Not for long," Ollie repeated, and I heard a dinging noise on his heart monitor. It had ticked up, rushing quickly into a range that meant something was wrong with him. Or that he was suddenly nervous. The analysts would try to find the root of his anxiety; where did it first begin to uptick, what was a personal triggering word for Ollie? Did this mean he actually knew something about the war Mei was building up to?

And promise me that you know me, the real me. You know I love this country and I love you, and I would give my dying breath to protect both. Ollie's words echoed through me, calming me while simultaneously shaking me. What did Ollie know?

He was uncomfortable now as he sat there. He was barely even focused. Something was going on, and Ollie knew it. The previous day, the vice admiral had said something about things happening very soon. That statement had made Ollie's entire demeanor shift. Were the two related? Mei Wang and Ping Zhao? What did time and war and Zhao have to do with Mei?

"The beast whom the Red Dragon was building a plan against was quickly stealing the world that was once his to claim. Effortlessly, the beast swallowed everything the Red Dragon had worked for, and those who followed the beast had wings just like him. The Red Dragon hated that everyone had caved to the beast for wings. No one worked hard anymore. At least that's what he thought until he met someone."

"Who'd he meet?"

"A follower of the winged beast. Yet, his wings were not given to him, they were earned. He was the only one in all of the world who'd submitted to the winged beast but was not simply given anything. The Red Dragon loved that and found that he loved the follower of the beast with the earned wings. The Red Dragon calls him a *saint*."

I stepped forward.

"Cool it," Hunter said quickly.

"This is crap, and you know it," I snapped at him.

"Remember your rank, lieutenant," General Hunter warned.

"Forget rank! Get the general out of there!"

"Hey!" Murphy shouted, silencing me and Hunter. "Who do you think you are, soldier? You don't get to—"

"Sir," one of the analysts interrupted the tongue lashing I was receiving from General Murphy, when he snapped his vision to her. "She just said that the Red Dragon is working with the saint. And together they are going to take down the winged beast."

All of us knew what she was implying, but none of us wanted to hear it. Most of all, I hoped that none of us believed it.

"Don't you want to know who the Red Dragon is? Who the saint and the winged beast are?" the woman asked.

"No," Ollie said flatly.

"I shall tell you anyway. The Red Dragon is among you. Left and right, he is there. His prey serve in his stead. And the winged beast is the bald eagle. And the saint," she smiled, crooked brown teeth and dark gums made me want to shrink away, but not any more than the implications she'd left in the air. "The saint, is you, Major General Claudius Saint-Olliare."

"Get him out of there!" I shouted.

Hunter agreed quickly. "Murphy, please get him—"

"Sir, his vitals are raging."

A thud came to the door, and Ollie was standing there. A worried look on his face. Shoving past the two generals, each trying to grip me, I ripped open the door.

"Keoni, you need to get out of here," Ollie said as he pulled me into his chest.

"They're coming," Mei whispered.

"Shut up!" I shouted, trying to break loose from Ollie. He fought against my struggling and pulled me close. "Ollie," I hiccuped in his arms.

"Listen to me," he said, cupping my chin. The room was in an uproar behind us, everyone shouting about what to do, and what to believe. Through burning tears, I looked up at Olliare. He was smiling, producing a glimmer of joy for my sake. For some reason, I felt like this was it. This was as far as the road went for Ollie and me. Any further, and neither of us would make it.

"I love you, Keoni. And I can't live without you. Everything I've done is for you, and I don't regret a thing. But I need you to run now."

"Run... run... the dragon will breathe out the sun. Run... run... the dragon is prepared to have fun. He will reign. He will rule. He will be the one to flatten the fool. Feel his envy, feel his fury, feel his majesty as you are buried." Mei pulled out a pill and popped it into her mouth.

"No!" I shouted as she began to foam and convulse at the table.

"Get out of here!" Ollie was shoving me back into the control room when shrieks rang out in the distance, the ringing of an alarm sounding off.

"Ollie, please don't make me go without you. I love you!"

"Go, Keoni!" He shoved me hard, and I stumbled backwards into the room as gunfire went off below us.

Scrambling to my feet, I reached for Ollie as I tried to lunge forward. But I was yanked back. Someone was yelling for me to get myself together as Ollie screamed that he loved me over the chaos.

The lights began to flicker, and all at once, the sound of whistling silenced all of us before my entire world went black.

18

Through You, O Gog, I Vindicate My Holiness Before Their Eyes

Zion

Thomas Jefferson once said, *God's justice will not sleep forever.* And because of that, he feared for his country. Today, I shared the same fear.

The news outlets covered the bloody and catastrophic battle for Israel after Russia and many surrounding countries invaded. However, things did not go as planned for the invaders, but they went exactly as Ezekiel detailed in chapter thirty-eight. The prophet mentioned that an earthquake would happen in Israel, and the whole earth would quake too.

For the longest, I thought that he meant the earthquake would begin in Israel, and the trembling would reach around the world. However, Ezekiel meant an earthquake would occur in Israel, and the devastation the invading forces will meet will shake the entire world. We will know that God is the one leading the invaders to a reckoning. And we will not forget it.

How could we? Israel, the chosen city of God to be a teacher to mankind was being invaded. They were completely surrounded, and yet, the only reports of bloodshed so far have been from the invaders. Drone footage has shown heaps of dead bodies in Russian uniforms, Turkish uniforms, Lebanese uniforms, all kinds except for Israeli uniforms.

God was fighting for Israel, He was protecting the land and its people, like He promised He would. Israel had become a battlefield overnight, and the battle was between the Russians with their invading team… and God. That message would've been received if we were all Believers.

The news had made a mockery of the invasion. Saying that Israeli forces are strong now because they've had time to prepare, but they believed they would soon fall. They said the Bible was scripted, false text to give people hope. The news anchors even laughed at the social media outcry of the 'Gog Magog War.' They said it was no different from Jesus.

God let His only Son get on the cross and die just for His own glory, and so He would bring Israel into war for His glory again. They criticized the Bible and called God selfish. They even mentioned a social media survey that asked how many people still identified as Christians after this invasion, and the number was significantly low.

A prophesy fulfillment is supposed to bring people closer to God. Something as old as the Bible being fulfilled was amazing, and yet, people were turning against God in droves.

Wrongly, they accused Him of 'using' Israel for His own gain. Criticizing that God had 'selfishly' picked Israel and never cared or fought for any other nation on Earth.

What had become of the world I lived in overnight? Was this truly the country I was training to serve? The country that sent no aid to Israel, yet mocked them and the God we supposedly trusted, according to what was written on our own money?

Despite the negativity it faced, God's Word was true, as It always had been. When He prophesied that His name would be vindicated, and that the nations would know Him, there was a fulfillment today. Every nation that wrongly accused God or twisted the Bible, had come to know of God because of this invasion, just like He said they would.

It was all too much happening at once. The dark teasing of Israel, the invasion of the Holy country, and Abbey having contractions all night. I woke to her aching in the bathroom. While I was gone, she didn't get the chance to turn the guest room into the baby room, so we'd spent my entire first day back decorating the room. And now I'm glad we did because her contractions haven't stopped since 1AM.

It started as a contraction every thirty to forty-five minutes. And then, they were coming more frequently, and Abbey could barely take it. Thankfully, she'd spent the time during the earlier contractions packing herself a bag for the hospital stay.

Our daughter was finally on the way, though a little early, and now, I had to tell my parents. I'd hidden Abigail's pregnancy for five and a half months. I never thought about what I'd do when the baby arrived—and now she's about to be here early. I'd have to tell my parents something. I didn't think I should hide it anymore in case Abbey needed help while I was away for the military. Besides, we were planning to get married, so I hoped they would be a little lenient on me.

"Are you ready?" I asked as I crossed back into the bedroom.

Abbey was sitting on the bed breathing deeply.

"Give me a second," she said.

Finding my way back out the room, I tried not think about telling my parents the truth, and the war in Israel. This war was all I needed to get myself to shift gears with God. The invasion of Israel meant the rapture was on the horizon. I did not want to be left behind, and I didn't want Abbey to be either. We needed to get things right, and we would after the baby got here.

Standing in the living room, I looked out the tall windows. I was just daydreaming, thinking of how much my life was about to change. A child running around and stopping to look out at the city of Springfield through these floor-to-ceiling windows. I'm sure she'll think that Springfield is the entire world, yet there's so much more out there for her to see.

I sighed at the sappy fatherly thoughts.

"What is happening to me?" I whispered as I stepped forward and placed a hand on the window. The sun had begun to rise, and normally the beauty of its horizon was one I liked to share with Abbey. But I gazed out and noticed the rising smoke obstructing the view of the horizon.

There was a building far off with a dark cloud billowing from it. I leaned closer, trying to figure out what I was looking at, when I noticed there were people in the streets. They were running and screaming. Just then, an explosion went off somewhere in the distance. There was a shopping center on fire now, traffic came to a halt and the city was spiraling out of control.

Pushing off the window, I raced for the remote and flicked on the television.

"America is under siege!" the anchor was screaming as he and the camera man raced down a dark alleyway. "America is under siege! We are being invaded! The—" the audio cut, and before the camera followed, the spotty footage showed a man in a US Army uniform tackling the reporter. I guess someone else tackled the camera man.

Something wasn't right. US soldiers attacking their own people?

Tossing the remote away, I went into the bedroom where Abbey was standing and pacing back and forth.

"We've got to go," I said as I pulled my gear from beneath the bed.

"I'm trying, Zion, but it hurts so—"

"Something's happening, Abbey, and I need to get you to safety."

Her contractions were suddenly less painful as she stood erect. "What's wrong?" She glanced at the gear in my hands. "Why do you need that?"

"I think there's been an attack on the city. I don't know, but we've got to get moving."

"Hold on, Zion. You need to tell me what's happening."

"Can I at least explain on the way?"

She sighed and nodded. Grabbing her hand, I slung my gear over my shoulder and grabbed her baby bag. We moved quickly down the hall and into the parking lot. The whole city was covered in a haze of smoke.

"What is going on?" Abbey cried as she looked around.

"Come on." I tugged on her hand as we moved toward the car. Once inside, I told her, "Hospitals are most likely full. I'm going to take you to my parents' house."

"What? *Now?*"

"I can't let you go to a hospital with an attack on the city. I need you to be somewhere safe so I'm not worried." I drove around a stopped car in the middle of the street. I was taking the back streets since I figured all the main ones were backed up.

"Not worried? Zion, where are you going to be?"

"I-I'm going to the armory," I said shamefully.

Abigail didn't speak.

"Baby, they need me." I reached for her hand, but she shoved it away.

"*I* need you, Zion!" she screamed at me. "I need you here! We're having a baby; doesn't that mean anything to you?"

"Of course, it does! That's why I'm taking you to my parents, so you'll be safe. I've just got to—" My phone rang, and Abigail screamed out, "Your stupid phone is always ringing!"

"I'm sorry," I apologized meekly as I pulled it out. Trying to stay focused on the road, I answered without seeing who it was. "Hello?"

"And you answered?!" Abigail snapped.

"Reinhardt!"

"Gabby?"

"Who is Gabby?" Abigail frowned.

"He's a comrade," I said to her quickly. "Gabby, what's going on?"

"China invaded! We need you here at the armory. Can you get here?"

"China did what?" I looked over at Abbey, her brows were knit together in confusion.

"They invaded, man, and it's bad. They're here in the city, already got the headquarters. No one knew we had a split headquarters except the US."

"So, it's an inside job," I said as I swerved the car. Veering onto my parents' street, I checked on Abbey who was holding her belly, aching again.

"We think so," Gabby answered.

"It's got to be. Did you see the news?"

"No, what happened? I got a call from Carter; he got me up to speed before I came in."

"The anchor and cameraman were both attacked by US soldiers."

"That was the same thing someone in Florida said." Gabby huffed, like he was rushing around. "Carter said his grandparents lived in Florida; they've got beach front property. Early this morning, old missile capsules showed up on shore, and there was even word that a submarine somewhere down the bay washed up. But the men who got out of these things were Chinese American men in US uniforms."

"They're attacking the coasts and the heart of the country." I shook my head as fear entrapped me. "Listen, I'm dropping my girlfriend off at my parents' place, then I'll be at the armory."

"We won't take to the streets until you get here. Come ready for battle."

"I will," I said before hanging up. Reyes Gabriel was always ready for battle. This excited him, I know. However, I was just trying to stay strong for Abbey's sake. "Come on," I murmured as we got out the car together. "Look, I haven't told my parents yet, but they'll be cool about it."

She shook her head, pain crippling her features. "I don't care," she said softly. "I just want you to come back. Please, come back, Zion."

I took her into my arms and held her. Taking in the minty smell from her shampoo, I nuzzled her big curls before kissing the top of her head.

"I love you, Abigail. And I promise I'll come back for you."

"I love you too." Getting to her tiptoes, she kissed my cheek, and headed for the front door. Watching her from the car, I saw the door open and my mother stare down at Abbey. My pregnant fiancée stepped aside to look back at me, and my mother's gaze was not cold. She was surprised, but she didn't let an ounce of disappointment or anger touch her face.

With a raised chin, she gave me a firm nod before bringing Abigail into the house.

— ÷ —

"Let's go! Let's go!"

Everyone was yelling at the armory. Most of us had our own gear, however, some didn't. Those who rushed here without any sort of weapon or equipment were sent to the basement where most of the weapons were held. I slipped by one of the tables of sergeants to change into my uniform and find Gabby. He'd told me that he hadn't reported to anyone yet. With everything so hectic, he was able to slip away to the second floor and hide until I got there.

"Gabby?" I called down the empty hall. A few minutes later, the creak of a door echoed down the hall, and he stepped out. "There you are man, why didn't you return any of my calls? I've been all the way down the hall the other way," I said as I jogged down to him. My pace slowed as I got closer, realizing Gabby was silent. His normally cheerful eyes were misting over now. Brown orbs melting into salty tears made my feet stop moving.

Looking him over in the dim light, I noticed there was blood dripping from one of his hands.

"Gabriel," I said firmly as I clutched my rifle, "what's wrong?"

He only stood there. Not answering. A tear rolled down his cheek, and instinctively I took a step back. Something was wrong. Something had happened…

"Carter! Grace!" I shouted.

No one answered.

My breathing picked up, and I could feel myself beginning to panic. One of the things they taught at bootcamp was how to avoid panicking, and it was to stay focused. Remember that someone is going to die if you don't get the job done, remember that your brothers in arms need you. And as I looked at Gabriel, a stilling breath calmed my nerves.

Think, I thought as I stared at Gabby. His hand was bleeding. He wasn't speaking, and he was crying. Typical of a hostage situation where the hostage couldn't talk. *The enemies are in that room.* Most likely aiming a gun at his head, or at Carter and Grace. If I made a rash move, I'd get someone killed, and likely myself too.

Think! I shouted within. *God, help me.*

Backing away from Gabby, I saw a raw panic wash over him. *I'm coming back, Reyes, don't worry.*

Turning away, I jogged back down the hall until I thought my footsteps couldn't be heard. Immediately, I pulled off my bags and lay them quietly on the floor. Strapping my rifle across my chest, I tucked a pistol in my leg holster and on my hip. I only had a few minutes to make this work if I wanted to rescue the guys, so I made quick work of unlacing my boots and setting them to the side.

I needed to be quiet when I headed back down the hall. They couldn't know I was there. I'd been trained in boots, but I was afraid with all the echoing in the hall, if I made one mistake, everyone would hear it.

Pulling my helmet on, I got to my feet and checked my sights before moving back down the hall. Each step was quieter than the last. Each one brought me closer to the door of death, but it also brought me closer to rescuing my brothers.

America had been betrayed by her own forces; no one knew who to trust anymore. Sure, it began with Chinese forces, but we had no idea how many allies they had now. This wasn't just the US versus China—it was the third World War.

Whatever the case, Gabby, Carter, Grace, and Diaz if he was here, could be trusted, and I would do anything to save them.

Halfway down the hall, I tapped my phone and called Gabby. I could hear his phone ringing from the room he was in, and the noise gave me a little leeway to move loudly.

"Gabriel?" I shouted. "Gabriel!"

I heard shuffling and got to the floor. When the door opened, a Chinese soldier stepped out, and I fired. The bullet hit him in the foot, and he hollered, crumbling to his knees. Jumping to my feet, I ran by him and tossed a gas canister into the room. When it burst, I pulled my mask up and goggles down and stepped inside. I could hear coughing and heaving and people moving as I peered around.

There was a struggle going on somewhere in the room, I could hear the grunts and sounds of a gruesome exchange. I moved in to find the struggle when the man I'd shot outside the door screamed, "He's inside! He's inside!"

I whirled around without thinking and fired again. This time, the bullet went through his head, silencing him permanently. With shaky breathing and chaos forming all around me, I stopped to stare at the man I'd just killed. I'd never killed anyone before. I'd shot live rounds plenty of times, but I'd never killed a single soul.

"Reinhardt! Watch out!"

A fire erupted in my lower back, sending me falling forward. I'd been shot. Thankfully, I had a vest on, but the pain was still unbearable. Writhing on the floor, I heard footsteps coming towards me. Fighting to turn over, I swung my gun to the front in just enough time to shoot the man coming at me. He gasped as he clutched his chest.

Stumbling backwards, I realized I'd shot a soldier. We were all soldiers. But I'd shot the *wrong* soldier. As the smoke dissipated, I ripped my goggles off. My eyes burned a little from the haze, but I was able to ignore all the pain as I got to my feet.

"Gabby?" I whispered as I stepped forward.

He was clutching his chest as he heaved.

"No…" I shook my head. "No, Gabby!" I screamed as he dropped to his knees, blood dripping from his mouth.

I began to panic as I looked around for help. There were bodies lying around... Grace's body, and Carter's. I looked around for the person who'd shot me when I saw a door connecting the two rooms swaying back and forth, as if it'd been swung open quickly.

"Ok..." I slid down to my feet and pulled out a first aid patch. Tearing it open, I said, "Gabby, hold this to your chest, alright? You're going to be okay. I've got to go find this guy. He can't get away."

I pressed the patch to his chest, but he didn't try to grab it. He just heaved, blood drooling down his chin, soaking his uniform. "I wanted... to fight," he struggled.

"Come on, Gabby! Don't say that!"

I tried to apply pressure, pushing the soaked padding harder into his chest. Reyes was weak, though, and we ended up falling back. I sat up and tried to apply pressure again, but it just made him spit blood at me involuntarily.

"Reyes, I'm sorry. Please don't do this."

Shakily, he reached up and clutched my shoulder with his bloody hand. "Thank you... for coming...back." His words were quiet as he struggled to speak.

"No, Reyes! We haven't joined the special forces together! We have to do it!" Tears fell from my eyes before I realized it.

"Join for me." He gurgled a little as he tried to chuckle. "I guess I didn't make the cut."

"Reyes..." I swallowed. No matter how much I shook my head, this was happening. He was dying because of me, and he didn't blame me. He wasn't even angry.

"I'm so sorry," I wept. "I'm so sorry!"

"Me too," he said quietly.

There was no reason for Gabby to apologize. If I hadn't been distracted, I could've saved him. We wouldn't be here if I hadn't been taken aback by death.

"Find that traitor," his voice called to me through struggled breathing. "Find him and... repay him."

"I will," I cried. "I will!"

He snorted, and then coughed harshly. "Please," he shook his head, "don't watch me die. I... don't want you... to remember me like this."

Swallowing, I nodded. "I won't watch, but I can't leave you."

Gabriel's chest began to rise quickly, and his body jerked with every rigid movement. Moving beside him, I lay there with my comrade, assuring him that I was there until the very end.

As his body riled beside me, my tears increased, and I could do nothing but lay there.

"I'm so sorry, Private Gabby."

19

I Will Enter into Judgement with Him

Zion

I don't know how long I stayed in that room with my dead comrades. I lined all their bodies up along the wall and checked to make sure they had their tags. Lying their jackets over their faces, I removed their nametags, and took the patches off their jackets so no one could impersonate them. I stared down at the American flag patch in my hand. Each one of my friends had fought hard to save this country, and I hoped I wouldn't be the only one to remember them.

"Private Valentin Carter, Private Martin Grace, and Private Reyes Gabriel, I won't sleep until I've avenged all three of you. I promise."

Thankfully, my things were still at the opposite end of the hall, where I'd left them. I flopped down beside my bag and stared at the wall. I killed my best friend in arms, though I had been trying to save him. I wasn't looking at faces, just at the uniform approaching. I thought it was the enemy soldier, not Gabriel. But it didn't matter because he was gone now. I was all alone.

Picking up the phone, I tried to call Abbey, but there was no answer. I didn't bother again since I knew she'd been having contractions all morning and had probably gone into labor by now. Checking my phone for texts, I realized more than a few hours had passed, an entire day had gone by while I'd laid there with my comrades. I'd fallen asleep. Though their slumber would never end, at least I'd slept with them for some time.

The troubling thoughts of Abbey not answering began to wrack my brain, but I tried to take comfort in knowing she was with my parents. If nothing else, they might've gotten her to a hospital by now. Maybe they just had bad reception. Or maybe Abbey was sleeping after having the baby. Maybe the labor took longer than expected.

With the world in chaos and phone lines probably down, anything was possible. But that was just it... *anything* could have happened to Abbey or to my parents. What would I do if I'd chosen to come fight and let my best friends die, and my fiancée? I couldn't stop my dark thoughts from fogging my mind now as I got my boots on.

Letting go of a breath, I slipped my phone into my back pocket and headed down the stairs. I'd decided to go back to my parents' house.

In the main foyer of the armory, there was a rush of soldiers like I was reliving yesterday. I pushed through them, squeezing by to reach the door when a sergeant called me.

"Hey! Where are you going? What platoon are you in?"

"I… I don't know, sir," I replied. "But my fiancée, I think she's in trouble and—"

"The whole city's in trouble! Your girlfriend doesn't mean a thing! Get your head on straight, soldier. If we let everyone with a loved one go, we'd be out of an army!"

"She's my *fiancée*!" I screamed.

"I don't care if she was your *wife*!" he fired back.

I was so worried and still shaken about Gabby and my friends that everything boiled over in one big shove. I shoved him back so hard, he stumbled into another guy before launching at me. We tussled for a moment, but it was mostly me trying to get free to go find Abbey.

"Hey! Hey! That's enough!" A man, at least six foot seven, with thick muscles beneath a blanket of silky dark skin came over and ripped us apart.

"Reinhardt?" he said.

"Sergeant Davis." I sighed with relief. He was one of the drill sergeants at camp, and the person who'd released me from Major Banks' rifle exercise.

"What's going on?" he asked, looking between the two of us.

The sergeant I was fighting with was the first to speak. "This private thinks his *fiancée*," he said nastily, "is more important than all of Missouri."

221

"That's not true," I shot back. "My fiancée was in labor yesterday, and I haven't heard anything from her. I couldn't get her to a hospital, so I left her with my parents. But no one's answering my calls now."

Davis nodded. "You know we're doing an evacuation right now. Signal could be lost because of that."

"I-I didn't know that."

Davis squinted. "Where have you been?" He looked me over, undoubtedly noticing the blood all over me.

"There was an enemy upstairs. I killed one, but the other got away."

"What?" Davis and the sergeant said in unison.

"Send two units upstairs," Davis said immediately to the sergeant, he nodded and took his leave.

"Tell me exactly what happened."

"Sir, I've already told you. I need to get to my fiancée."

Davis stirred. "Give me the details and I can release you with a unit that's going to be heading in the direction of where you want to go."

"Thank you, sir," I nodded.

I took a breath as I recalled the traumatic events from yesterday. "I went upstairs looking for Private Reyes Gabriel, he'd told me to come to the armory and was waiting for me so we could be assigned to the same unit."

"And then what happened?"

"When I got up there, he stepped out of the room, but he was crying, and bleeding. And I knew something was wrong."

"Hostage situation?"

222

"Yes, sir," I confirmed. "I retreated down the hall and removed all my loud gear and shoes and went back to save him." Pausing, I tried to think of a way to tell Davis that I'd accidentally killed Gabriel, but a big slap to my back jerked me forward.

"You did great. I'll get this information to our communications team." He looked at his watch and then said, "The next unit is heading out in ten minutes. You can go with them, or you can wait and see what unit is heading in your direction."

"I'll go now. Thank you, sir."

I took off towards the exit to find the unit that was readying to do a sweep and survey. We were taught at bootcamp that a sweep and survey unit went out to locate bodies and civilians who might've missed an evacuation call.

Gunfire still wailed outside, and I knew the invasion was far from over. After checking in with my platoon sergeant, we took to the streets of Springfield to begin a sweep and survey on the northside. My parents lived on the southern outskirts of Springfield, but I didn't care. I was counting on the chaos to break free from the unit and hike it to my parents' place.

Our platoon stepped into the chaos of the invasion, running in unison. We would be splitting into teams of eight, each team taking a street to sweep and survey casualties. I hadn't been outside in a single day, and yet it looked like the entire world was falling apart. Cars were turned over; small fires danced everywhere. Buildings were crushed or swallowing cars that'd rammed into them. The blood that raced to the drains seemed like it would never stop flowing. Our boots made imprints in the crimson streets as we trucked along.

If an invasion of one city with a small army caused this much destruction, how much more had Israel seen with several nations invading at once? I shook my head, trying to stay focused. I couldn't let my mind wander. I needed to pay attention, watch for an opening, watch for the right moment to slip away, and find my way back to Abbey and my parents.

My eight-man team split off to hike up a street and begin surveying. Each member took a section of the street to clear, and I raced to the top of the street. If I lingered long enough, I could get away, and circle back south. I stood by a house with two cars in the driveway, clutching my rifle as I moved closer.

I would at least check one house before leaving. Inching forward with my rifle aimed, I climbed the steps and pushed through the half open door. It was a mess inside, like some kind of struggle had happened. It could've been anything, honestly. People searching for things to take with them during the evacuation. Or maybe a traitor got inside and struggled with the inhabitants. There was blood on the carpet of the living room, giving me my answer.

Keeping my rifle lifted, I walked quietly through the house, hoping to surprise anyone still here. The pristine white furniture in the living room reminded me of Abigail. She loved things like that. There was a flight of stairs with pictures hanging on the walls. I glanced at them as I moved up the stairs until I recognized the woman in the pictures.

"Major Banks?" I whispered. The wall was lined with photos of her and a man smiling and laughing on Thanksgiving. The décor on the frame said, 'Our First Thanksgiving.' She looked happy; they both did.

I gulped down my nerves, hoping I wouldn't find the major dead somewhere in the house. I picked up the pace as I raced up the rest of the stairs of the quiet house. I cleared the bathroom, and the spare bedroom. I crept to the end of the hall where I assumed the master bedroom was.

Taking a breath as I stood outside the door, I quickly opened it, and pointed my gun inside. There was a stench, a *foul* one. One I smelled here, but never smelled on my comrades. It was probably because I'd been in the room when they'd died, or maybe all the heightened emotions kept me from smelling anything. But there was nothing obscuring my sense of smell now as death roved over my nose.

There was blood on the floor, a lot of it. Like whatever started downstairs was finished up here. Drags marks were on the white carpet, but the man in bed looked like he was asleep.

"Sir," I called.

Swallowing, I came around the bed and gasped. I let my rifle sag around my neck as I tripped backwards, staring at the body. It was the man from the pictures. He was lying still, hands at his side like he was asleep. Yet, his throat was cut open. There was red tape on his face that should have kept his mouth closed, but the tendons in his jaw on both sides had

225

been severed, allowing it to sag open and bleed into the pillow his head rested on. There were other markings and gashes on his arms and hands, bruises on his face, indicating there had been a struggle or a fight.

I looked around the room for clues, wondering why this death had been so intentional, so personal. And then I found it. On the headrest above the man, the phrase, **Silence Exchange,** was carved. I didn't know what it meant, but I knew it wasn't good. I hated being the one who found the house, now I'd have to be the one to tell the major if I ever saw her again.

Down the stairs and out of the house, I spotted the team making their way down the street. I jogged to the end of it when I felt my phone buzzing. I stopped on a dime and whipped it out. It was Abbey. Relief washed over me, but it was quickly chased away when a piercing scream broke out. Looking for who the voice belonged to, I found a woman backing away from a man. He was tall and buff looking. But so was she. It looked like she could take him if she tried. But she must've seen something I couldn't see because she was screaming for her life as she scooted across the concrete, slamming right into a car.

The man wobbled as he walked. Tripping left and right, like he couldn't get his footing. Shoulders hunched, and his head hung low, the man stumbled towards the screaming woman.

"Sir!" I yelled. "Sir!"

He stopped at once. Jerking his head to the side before craning his neck to see me.

"What is—"

The man screeched and ran towards me. He was abnormally fast. Running at a speed that startled me. Even with the distance between us, I didn't think I could outrun him. As he got closer, I lifted my rifle and fired.

He kept running.

I panicked. Backing away now, I began to scream for help as I unloaded a magazine into his chest. It didn't stop him. He jerked backwards from the force of the bullets, but his legs kept moving. Even as he was peppered with shots.

This was certainly no man at all. Something else had invaded our home. Some other force had joined this confusing fray. An army of unstoppable men was roaming the streets. And one of them was running right at me.

It's going to kill me if I don't kill it first.

The thought sent a jolt of electrifying fear raging through my body. Shakily, I grabbed a smoke bomb off my hip and threw it. It exploded, giving me a few moments to turn and run.

"Help! Help!" I shouted.

A female soldier raced from a nearby house with her gun raised. "There's something dead in there!" she hollered, wearing a panicked expression I'm sure matched my own.

The creature screeched behind me, and when I looked back, it had cleared the smoke, racing right towards me.

"Shoot it!" I screamed.

227

The soldier stood there in awe; her weapon now lowered. "Shoot! Shoot!"

Behind her, another soldier took aim and fired. Falling to the ground, I turned over to find the creature inches away from me. It was lying face down, but even so, I could tell something was wrong. The skin was sagging, and the body looked rugged.

"W-Wh-What is that!?" I screamed.

"I don't know," Private Winston said as he came over. Grabbing me by the hand, he pulled me to my feet. My legs wobbled and I could barely stand.

"Thank you," I panted.

There was no telling what I was looking at. There was no telling what had chased me. I couldn't describe it as anything other than a creature, some type of monster thing with incredible agility and resistance to bullets. The petrifying screeches and the horror of its appearance was something of a nightmare. Except it was reality, and I was hoping I'd wake up.

"One of those things was in the house I checked," the female soldier told us. "It had a bullet in its head, and bullets all over its body. Like someone had tried to kill it, but it wouldn't die."

"I unloaded an entire magazine into this one." I was still panting as I tried to gather my thoughts on what had just happened.

"Come on," Winston said, "let's move."

I nodded, following behind the older man. He was only a private because he was a draftee. I remembered him from training. He'd always been quiet, nothing much to say, but he was pretty smart.

Winston and I headed down the street in the opposite direction, gathering Sam—the female soldier—and the rest of the team. Our plan was to head back to the armory and explain what we'd seen. I was alright with waiting to go see Abbey since she'd called me back, and I knew she was safe. However, if one of those things were to get to her and our daughter, I wouldn't be there... could I really live with that? But what about my duty, my comrades? I couldn't just leave them now with these things everywhere. We needed to stick together, traveling alone was too dangerous.

God, please, I'm begging You to protect Abbey until I can get to her... Please.

20

Have You Come to Seize Spoil?

Claudius

America has fallen. I was supposed to be upset. I was supposed to be angry. But all I felt was worried. As young privates, we're taught that our feelings don't matter, only the mission at hand. But I'd chosen Keoni once when we'd been fooling around in secret. And I'd chosen her again—this time in public, screaming that I loved her in front of everyone.

America's invasion was a dark night that wouldn't see a horizon anytime soon. And because of that, I had to find Keoni. I had to save her and tell her the truth I didn't get the chance to say before.

Deep within my heart, I'm forcing myself to continue in this unhinged obsession with Keoni. If, for a second, I let myself realize what I've done to the nation, to the balance of the entire world, I don't think I could make it.

There was an explosion somewhere in the joint force headquarters building a day ago that sent the interrogation room down to the level below it. When I drifted back to consciousness after the explosion and the fall, I was able to get outside—but my leg was broken, and I couldn't go very far. I wanted to find Keoni, of course, but all I'd managed to do after getting away from headquarters was lock myself inside the shed of someone's backyard.

There was no food or water inside, just tools and motor oil. It took me most of yesterday to make a makeshift stabilizer out of tent pegs and tape for my leg. Adjusting against the wall, I sighed. I could die here or take the risk of making my leg worse. Either way, it wasn't going to be easy to get out of here.

The explosion at the headquarters surprised all of us. When Zhao told me that America would be invaded, I never thought it would happen so soon, even after his visit to my office the night before the invasion. But it made sense. Seeing as Zhao had those security system errors, and he knew that our station in Springfield was split with Washington, launching an attack here had to be part of his plan all along. But was he the coordinator of the Red Dragon? He couldn't be.

I'd heard of the Red Dragon once before during a mission in Syria. It was just a fable, I thought. But the story was eerily similar to the one that old hag spewed in the interrogation room. I don't think Zhao's the mastermind behind the terrorist group, but he played a huge role. At least he played a big role in my incrimination. Which is why I'm on the run. My incrimination is why I needed to get to the cabin and tell Kiki the truth.

I tried not to let thoughts of Keoni and this invasion send me into a spiraling depression. Instead, I checked my surroundings again. I'd broken through a small wooden gate and got into this old shed right after waking up from the explosion. Thankfully, my watch was still working so I was able to keep track of time. I didn't need it, though, since this shed was kind of shabby.

A little sunlight peeked in through the wooden planks of the walls, and I was able to keep track of time that way too. I wasn't out for too long after the explosion, I suspected. Though I hadn't been looking at my watch when the explosion occurred, it was early morning when I was called in for the interview. It's been a day now, and I didn't want to spend another night in this shed.

I checked around for another exit other than the door I'd entered through. The small shed only had one door, unfortunately, as it was filled with all kinds of junk. Motor oil, bags of car tools, extension cords—there was even something that looked like some kind of lever. It was detached from whatever it'd initially been attached to, but whoever used the old, ragged shed knew a thing or two about cars.

As I was contemplating how to get out of here, I heard a noise outside. I stiffened, listening to the rustling of the grass. It sounded like footsteps; someone was approaching the shed. I reached for the tool bag and dragged it over to pull out a wrench. My plan was to throw it first, and then grab something else from the bag. It was the best I could do with a broken leg. I wasn't going to die without a fight.

"Is someone in there?" The voice was small, childish even.

I clutched the wrench in silence. No one could be trusted. The voice may sound young, but who knew what was on the other side. I heard the lock click, and my stomach nearly jumped into my mouth as I readied myself. The big door was pulled open to reveal an actual child. A little girl was standing there holding a big shotgun.

"Whoa!" I called, dropping the wrench immediately. "Put that thing down, okay?"

"King told me to use it if something happened while she was gone."

"King?" I swallowed. "Who's King?"

"My sister," she huffed as she lowered the gun.

What an interesting name for a sister...

I watched the small child struggle to lift it again and take aim. The gun looked heavy, too heavy for her at least.

"What's your name?" I asked, trying to distract her.

"Lyla," she said.

"Lyla, I'm a general in the military—"

"Coco said everything is the military's fault."

Whoever Coco is ... Screw you.

I resisted the urge to roll my eyes as Lyla continued to struggle with the gun. "Well, then I'm not in the military. I'm just playing dress up, and I hurt my leg."

Lyla took a small step forward to see my full body. Her small brown eyes looked without fear or worry. This little girl was just following orders her sister, King, had left her. As far as I could tell, she was doing a good job. If she could actually hold the gun, she might've been more intimidating.

"Lyla," I got her attention again, "let me show you how to hold the gun."

She backed up, shaking her head, but I shrugged, trying to be even nicer.

"Come on, it's heavy, right? I can show you how to make it a little lighter."

"Will you give it back?"

"I promise. Besides, what could I do with it? My leg's hurt, remember?"

She looked at my leg and then at me and nodded. Slowly, she lowered the gun with a sigh. I waved her on as she took cautious steps towards me. Tiny hands passed me the gun from a safe distance.

"First thing you have to know when holding a gun like this, is the recoil. You know what recoil is?"

She shook her head.

"Well..." I frowned. "Maybe that's not too important to know right now. Anyways, when you're holding a gun like this, you want to put all the weight against your body, right in the chest area. Like so." I whipped the gun up quickly, taking aim at the wooden wall ahead of me.

Lyla gasped and clapped like the little girl she was. I'd place her around six or seven, though from her tiny size I wouldn't be surprised if she was younger than that.

"You like that?"

"Yes!" she cheered.

I nodded, thankful she was so easy to entertain. If things continued to go well, I'd be able to get her to help me.

"See, if you let the gun sag, it'll make you tired." I lifted the gun quickly again and she squealed with glee. "But when you hold it snug against your shoulder, you can balance the weight and fire off some good rounds."

"Shoot! Shoot!" she exclaimed.

"Now, now, Lyla. If I shoot, then I'll put a hole in your shed. I can't shoot here."

"You can shoot out there." She turned and pointed to the gate I'd broken open to get in here. "King said there are people and monsters out there. That's why I couldn't go." She looked sad with her little mouth pulled into a frown.

"Monsters," I chuckled, "yeah, people can be monsters. But I can't go shooting like this. I need help. Food, water, a new splint." I pointed at my leg. "If you help me, we can go find some monsters to take out. You want to fight the monsters, right?"

"Mmhmm."

"Me too. I can do it if you help me."

Little Lyla danced for a moment, bouncing from one foot to the other as she thought this through. "Inside, there's food and water," she said slowly.

"Really? Can I have some?"

She nodded feverishly.

"Why don't you go make some food, and I'll come inside."

"Ok. And you'll play with me too?"

I paused. Then I thought, whatever, I need help. If I've got to play with a kid to get it, then fine.

"Yes!" I exclaimed as excitedly as I could.

"Ok! I am going to make you food like Coco!" She turned and ran from the yard to the white and red house.

With a deep sigh, I leaned my head back against the wall. I was thankful, so incredibly thankful that it was a little girl who found me and not an adult. With the gun in hand, I rummaged around, looking to piece something together for a crutch. The closest thing was a pole and two rags. I folded the rags on top of each other and taped them to the pole. After several standing attempts, and injuring myself further from all the falls, I got the pole beneath my arm. Jamming it into the ground, I hopped on the other leg until I made it to the door.

A toasted bagel with ham and cheese on it. That was all Lyla could cook since her sisters only let her use the toaster when they were gone. She had three older sisters; Acoye, who she called 'Coco' [screw her still]. Then there was Kingsley, the sister she always called 'King.' And finally, Chemistry. I assumed Chemistry was the oldest since Lyla sometimes referred to her as her mother.

The four sisters have been living alone for the past four years, right after Chemistry finished college. Lyla's only five, so she couldn't recall much about her parents. To her, Chemistry really was her mother. The story goes, as far as Lyla knows, that there was some kind of accident, and *her* mother was killed, and *their* father never returned.

I was sitting beside Lyla, who was lying on the floor coloring and talking. Periodically, I just agreed with whatever she said, but I wasn't listening. I was planning. Since Lyla didn't know when her sisters would return—they were out shopping is what she'd said, but I wasn't sure what she really meant by that since there was an invasion going on. I figured it was code for looting which meant I had limited time to figure out a game plan.

I could put Lyla to bed, take some supplies and start making my way to the cabin. Hopefully, Keoni would still be there. It'd been a full day, and I had no idea if she was alright or not, but I figured she was. The explosion happened below the interrogation room, and I only limped away with a broken leg. Keoni was probably fine and was probably taken to a hospital to be examined. After that, there were some protocols she would follow and then be able to go home. Though, with an invasion going on, it was likely none of that had happened at all.

Keoni could be lying in a pile of rubble. Or she could have stumbled out of HQ like me and escaped on foot. If authorities found her, she'd probably be taken in for questioning considering everything that'd happened before the explosion. If that was the case, she'd have to sneak away, and who knew how long that could take.

"Lyla," I started. Big brown eyes looked up at me from her coloring book. "Do you have a car?"

"They took it."

"Your sisters?"

"Mmhmm. We only have one."

"Do you—"

The front door opened, and I heard the young voice of a girl call out, "Lyla! We're back!"

"Coco!" Lyla exclaimed. "I'm in here!"

Lyla had let me keep the shotgun. I told her I would need it to shoot at the monsters when we went out later. But that was a lie, of course. I wanted the gun in case her sisters came back and tried to put me out. With a broken leg I was weak, but my desperation to find Keoni kept me from being pathetic and giving up.

Loud footsteps jogged through the house before a smiling girl, nearly identical to Lyla, rounded the corner. The girl froze, blinking from me to Lyla. I was sitting beneath a blanket, clutching the shotgun in case she made a sudden move.

Her smile faded, and her dark brows meshed together on her tawny-brown skin. "Kingsley, Chemistry! Come quick!" she exclaimed.

I swallowed as I heard the rushing footsteps of the two sisters. The girl, who I assumed was Coco, waved Lyla on and told her to come here. Putting down her crayon, Lyla obeyed her sister and went to her for a hug. Coco didn't stop staring at me. Her eyes were wide in fear, but her sisters caught my attention.

"Who are you!?" one of them shouted as she raised a pistol at me.

They'd stopped in their tracks, all three of the older sisters. One aimed a gun at me, the other protectively pulled her two sisters behind her. Clearly, Chemistry and Kingsley were the older two sisters. I didn't use my shotgun, instead, I threw my hands up defensively, trying to work things out civilly.

"Wait a second," I said calmly, "I'm not trying to hurt anyone."

"Who are you!" the girl with the pistol shouted again. She wasn't so much of a girl as she was a young woman. She reminded me of Keoni, with her warm brown skin and amber eyes. She had dreadlocks, long and thick, that reached her waist, as opposed to Keoni's short hair.

"Stop it!" Lyla ripped free from Coco and collapsed onto me. Thankfully, the gun was beside me and not in my lap, or that could've been a bad accident.

Wrapping an arm around the small girl as I took in the shock on each one of their faces, I said, "Lyla and I are friends." I needed to be on their good side if I wanted this to work out. This was already a kink in my plans. I was initially hoping to leave before they showed up, but now that they're here, I'd have to figure out a way to get them to let me stay or at least send me on my way peacefully.

"Who do you think you are!" the pistol girl nearly screamed.

"Stop it, Chemi! Cloud and I are friends!" little Lyla whined in my arms—she'd started calling me Cloud because it was easier to say than Claudius.

"Get off of him," Chemistry barked. "We told you to stay put and not let anyone inside! He could've killed you!"

"Cloud needed help! I saw him hide in our shed the other night, and I went to save him." Lyla fired back. I had no idea anyone had seen me, but I was grateful it was Lyla and not Chemistry … who was still aiming a gun at me.

"Chem," their other sister, Kingsley, finally spoke. Her voice was rich and womanly. "You're aiming a gun at our sister."

Begrudgingly, Chemistry lowered her gun.

"Who are you?" Kingsley asked in a much calmer tone than Chemistry.

"My name is Claudius."

"Why were you hiding in our shed?" Kingsley asked as she stepped forward. She reached for Lyla, who took her hand and climbed from my lap.

"I got hurt and that was the first place I found to hide."

"You didn't come inside then, but you found it alright to enter our house with a little girl? She's five years old!" Chemistry exclaimed. Her eyes were filled with anger, like she would beat me to death if it wasn't for Lyla.

"I know," I said apologetically. "And I'm sorry. It was wrong of me. But I thought I'd just be there for a night. I didn't think anyone would come looking for me today. I had no idea someone even saw me. I was just trying to get to safety. I'm sorry."

A stiff moment passed with Chemistry looking me over. "Kingsley, take them and get the rest of the supplies out the car. Put Lyla in the bedroom."

"I don't want to go!" Lyla exclaimed. "I want to stay with Cloud!"

Before Chemistry could shout at her baby sister, I said kindly (hoping to earn points with the sisters), "We'll go fight the monsters sometime later."

Lyla smiled. "You promise?"

"I do."

She sprung free from her sister and hugged me. "Ok, bye, Cloud."

"Bye, Lyla."

Kingsley took her by the hand, eyeing me an extra moment with Acoye on her heels before she left the room.

Checking over her shoulder, Chemistry faced me again. "Who are you and why are you here?"

"My name is Claudius Saint-Olliare, I'm a general in the US Army. I got mixed up in an accident, and my leg's broken. So, I took shelter in your shed." I pulled the covers back, careful to hide the shotgun, and revealed the homemade splint.

"I know who you are," Chemistry said flatly. "You're the missing major general, wanted for a big prize for treason against the United States."

"What?" I snapped. "*Treason?* I didn't do anything."

"The news said they couldn't find your body in the pile of rubble from that military headquarters. You're a wanted man, endangering my entire family."

241

"I swear I didn't do a thing. The news is *lying*. They've got the story twisted."

"So why are you running?"

I stammered for words.

Chemistry squatted in front of me and ripped the blankets off. She glared at the shotgun before looking up at me. "The only reason I haven't killed you is because of Lyla. I don't know what the truth is, and I don't care. But I'm willing to help you."

"What?" I was floored by her words. But her callous expression told me there was more to what she was saying.

"We have supplies, shelter, and a car. With the invasion still going, and those monsters roaming around, we can stay safe. But you won't need us once you're better. So I want you to remember our kindness."

"Monsters? What are you talking about?" I thought Lyla had been talking childish gibberish, but Chemistry is talking about monsters now too. And she's clearly not a child. She's clearly not insane.

"What's going on out there?" I asked. I'd only been in that shed for one day. What else could have possibly happened in 24 hours?

Chemistry glanced away, like remembering the monsters would give her an ulcer. "People dropped dead. Right in front of us. All at once. And some children vanished into thin air. Left nothing but their clothes behind. And then…" She looked back at me, eyes rounded in fear. "The ones who left their bodies behind? They came back to life."

"What?"

She shook her head. "I don't even know what I saw. And it doesn't matter because we are staying inside. So, you'll owe us." Her voice hardened again like she'd forced the thoughts of her chaotic story away.

I wanted to believe her, but it seemed so farfetched, I figured this must've been some kind of metaphor I wasn't picking up. *Maybe she's in shock,* I thought. *Maybe she doesn't have the story altogether.*

"Ok, I'll owe you," I agreed.

"Good." She stood and turned for the hall when I said, "Thank you."

Chemistry turned back, her dreads flowing behind her. "Sit on those thank you's and keep a good count. You'll need to remember how many you've said and repay me for each one."

I paused. "I get it. I'll owe you. It'll probably take a full month of recovery before I'm even walking again. Longer until I'm running. I'll owe you more supplies than I can gather alone. The only thing that would amount to my debt is the prize for turning me in."

She nodded.

"Very well."

Chemistry said nothing else as she left.

If the invasion warred on, then I wouldn't have to worry. In a month my name would probably be cleared, if not forgotten. There would be no prize for turning me in. Our economy was already struggling. If I waited this out, I could walk away from this perfectly healed up, *without* paying my debt. But Chemistry didn't need to know that.

21

To the Beasts of The Field to Be Devoured

Keoni

I've ridden in a tank, and Humvees, safari trucks, and other military vehicles. However, I have never ridden in an armored van. It was bullet proof all over. The van was specialized for transporting city officials, so there were tinted bullet proof windows as well. They were only there for decoration, so when the officials arrived, all the bystanders could wave to the important people inside.

Unfortunately, no one was waving to me. Not that I cared. I was being transported from the hospital to the main armory to help with organization and whatever else. While in the hospital, I was told that Ollie had gotten away, and that he was wanted for treason. I argued and fought for him, telling them that my superior was no traitor. Surprisingly, Hunter disagreed. He was supposed to be a good friend of Ollie's, but he didn't

245

stand for him. I was alone, fighting for the love of my life while trying to remember my duty to this fallen country.

I'd forgotten my duty to my country months ago when I reencountered Ollie. I let my loyalty to my country be smothered by a weeping desire to be with Claudius. I'd thought that was the right thing to do. I thought choosing love, choosing *Ollie*, was the right thing to do. But now, the country was being invaded and Ollie was nowhere in sight.

I am guilty of the invasion. If I'd taken my new rank, my new privileges, more seriously, maybe this all could've been avoided. Who can truly say, though? I criticized myself, but to the world, I was an innocent party.

They took my statement at the hospital but didn't find me guilty of anything but possibly insubordination. However, the evidence of that was up in flames around the city, and that wasn't important anymore. China had officially invaded the United States of America. Our forces weren't ready. They didn't take long to retaliate, but the initial shock of an invasion on American soil had to be accepted first. And that was no small pill to swallow. Not to mention the strange reports we'd gotten while I was in the hospital.

Children vanishing. Millions of people around the country dropping dead. All at once. It sounded like the makings of a horrible apocalypse movie.

In a single day, the country I'd fought for began to crumble, and the man I was going to marry had vanished. Initially, I wanted to get to the cabin or find Ollie if he wasn't there. But, after a day of interrogations and an overnight stay at the hospital for a bruised rib and a few scrapes, I still wasn't on my way to find Ollie. And that was a good thing. I needed to refocus, needed to remember my duty to this country since I'd forgotten for too long.

We were soldiers. I knew the mission had to come first, and I would do my very best to keep the mission first and my feelings second. Though, putting Ollie on the backburner while he was currently missing was hard. It was difficult to compartmentalize him in my mind when I had so many questions. It was hard when Ollie knew something, and he didn't get the chance to tell me. I never once questioned his innocence, but I did question what exactly he knew about this invasion. With him not here to tell me, I'd figure it out for myself.

A woman had come into HQ and asked specifically for Ollie, indicated him as a betrayer, and then proceeded to kill herself just moments before the invasion. Meanwhile, Ollie had been acting strange since the day before the invasion. It started with that tense exchange between him and the vice admiral.

Secretly, I wondered if Zhao knew something about this too. His odd behavior, his dark words before storming off from the meeting and never returning. And what made matters worse, Zhao was missing too. It was reported that he came into work early and went into his office and never came out. His office was checked, he wasn't there. No windows were left open, and the spotty footage didn't show him leaving his office or coming in.

It was possible the reports were fake. Zhao may have never come in at all, but if he didn't, it begged the question of why not. Did he know this was going to happen? There were too many questions burning my mind, too much to think about.

With a deep and exhausted sigh, I closed my eyes. The bumpy ride from the hospital was long, but the soldier driving the vehicle had just told me were getting close. Still had a little way to go, but it wouldn't be too long from now. I wished he could hurry. The sooner we got there, the sooner I could check in, and see what needed to be done.

All of Springfield was singed. Burning buildings, screaming people. There was nothing beautiful about the place anymore. China had left our home in shambles and was moving on to wreak havoc in the rest of the country. There was no telling how far north or south, east or west the Chinese forces would go, but we would stop them. We had too.

The humming of the truck was interrupted with bumps as we trudged over debris. There were no more smooth streets. China hadn't left a stone unturned.

Just as I leaned my head against the dark window, a loud thud hit the van.

"What was that?" I asked, sitting up quickly.

"Not sure," the soldier said nonchalantly. "We're safe though, whatever it was. Might've been a bird or something."

"We're at war, it could've been a bullet." My words came out with an edge I hoped was sharp enough to cut down his nonchalance.

"Sorry, lieutenant colonel."

I exhaled, clutching my gun nervously as I looked out the window. Something felt off. Something wasn't right.

Just then, another thud hit the vehicle.

"Did you see anything?"

"No, but I think it's—" His words were exchanged for a shriek as something crashed into the windshield.

The truck swerved, and I gripped the handle on the door.

"Calm down! We're fine!" I screamed.

The truck continued to swerve and, shakily, I shoved my gun into its holster and braced for impact. We rammed into something, throwing me forward and backwards as the van settled against whatever it had hit.

Sucking for breath, I clutched my side as pain ricocheted through my ribcage. "Hey," I called. "Hey!"

The soldier was slumped over the steering wheel. We'd been hit hard, but I knew he wasn't dead. With stiff movements, I climbed to the front and shook the soldier until he awakened.

"Get up," I said as he took a deep breath.

Blinking back the fuzziness, the soldier, Sergeant First Class Poyer, looked me over in confusion before he spoke. "What did we hit?"

"I don't know, but we've got to get out and see."

"Right." Unhooking his seatbelt, he followed me out the van and into the streets.

I stepped out with my gun raised, looking for an enemy. There was a burning haze that activated the tears in my eyes. Pushing through the pain, I checked around for what could've hit the truck as we circled the vehicle. It was rammed pretty good into an already destroyed building.

"I don't see anything," Poyer said behind me.

"Me either." I stopped walking and turned in a circle. "Something's not right. Something hit us and threw us off the road, and now it's silent out? Not even any gunfire in a city that's being invaded?"

"I agree. This is kind of—"

"Shh." I held up a hand. "Do you hear that?" I glanced back at Poyer. Blonde brows were raised as he shook his head. "You don't hear that noise. It sounds like it's getting closer."

"I think I do hear it now, like a screech?"

"Yeah."

We stood there for a moment, glancing in every direction until I spotted something running right at us. It looked like a human ... but not really. Like the frame was human, however, what was inside of the human frame was not human in any way.

With its head back, screeching a piercing noise, the creature jetted towards Poyer and me.

"What is that?" Poyer asked as he stepped beside me.

Raising my gun, I fired two shots at it. But the creature didn't slow down. It kept running. In fact, it seemed to get wilder and faster, running full force, with bare feet and arms dangling at its side.

"Run!" I shouted as I took off in the opposite direction of the creature. I raced for a building down the street. It must've been a school or something, because beside it was a playground.

As I sprinted, I checked over my shoulder for Poyer, he was running slow, and it dawned on me that he might've injured his leg in the car accident.

"Come on, Poyer! We've got to move!" I called back.

"I can't run! I'm trying!"

"RUN! That is an order!" I shouted before I picked up the pace. Ahead, there was a group of young soldiers jogging right towards me, and behind me was something chasing Poyer and me. "Run!" I screamed at the soldiers. "Run!"

They didn't listen. It was like they knew why I was shouting and had come to rescue us. For a moment, I felt relieved. But then I looked back and saw that Poyer had fallen.

"No!" I shouted, turning on my heels. I was racing time and that creature to get to him.

"Keoni! Don't!"

At the sound of my name, I glanced back at the approaching soldiers. Zion Reinhardt. He was running towards me, but the howling cry of the creature ripped my attention back to Poyer who was struggling to move.

"Get up, Poyer!" I screamed. "Get up!"

He shouted, reaching for me as the creature jolted into the air and came down clumsily on Poyer. It began to bite him … to—to *eat* him.

The horrible shrieks that came from Poyer drowned out my own screaming as Zion tackled me to the ground. Another soldier zipped by, shooting the creature in the head that was eating Poyer.

"Poyer!" I screamed.

He was lying there, stiff and lifeless.

"Come on," Zion panted as he tried to pull me to my feet.

"We can't leave him! We have to…" I trailed off as Poyer began to tick. His body jolted, riled, and jerked around before snapping completely in two. There was an audible cracking noise as the back of his head dragged against the street, folding to meet his feet and breaking his back.

"Poyer…?" I whispered.

"We gotta go!" The soldier who'd shot the first creature, was already beside me, helping Zion pull me to my feet.

I watched over my shoulder as they rushed me to the school building. The man who was once Poyer was now standing completely erect. A disheveled uniform, and his limbs looked elongated, like suddenly, they were all free of their joints and sockets. His head rang in a circle, his body twitched uncontrollably before releasing a hollering cry into the heavens.

Poyer was now one of those creatures… like he had somehow come back from the dead.

I can't believe this… I stared at the creature as it began to chase us down.

The United States has been invaded. The love of my life is missing and now marked as a traitor to the nation. Millions of people have dropped dead out of nowhere. Children have vanished into thin air. And the dead bodies left behind by those millions have risen again. And now they're trying to eat us.

This is not the war I signed up for.

Continue the series...

Ordained Catastrophe Book II: The Rise of Desolation

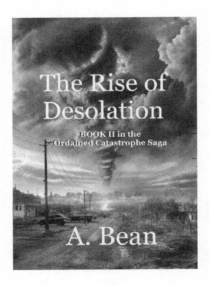

Coming July 16, 2023

More books by A. Bean & TRC Publishing!

Christian Fantasy
Cross Academy series
The End of the World series
The Scribe

Christian Post-Apocalyptic Fiction
The Barren Fields

Christian Science Fiction
I AM MAN series

Christian Romance
The Living Water
Withered Rose Trilogy
Fractured Diamond
The Woof Pack Trilogy
Singlehood

Christian Children's Fiction
Too Young

ACKNOWLEDGEMENTS

Jesus is the Christ, Son of the Living God.

I am thankful to God for giving me the idea for this novel. Thank You Lord for blessing me to complete Your assignment!

Thank you, the reader, who made it this far. You are awesome. I hope you take the time to read some of my other work and finish this series. It's been quite a journey already, hasn't it? Let's go on another.

Follow me on Amazon to get updates on new releases, pre-orders, and reduced prices on my books. Also, follow TRC on TikTok! We love meeting readers and discussing new ideas. See you there!

The Rebel Christian Publishing

We are an independent Christian publishing company focused on fantasy, science fiction, and romantic reads. Visit therebelchristian.com to check out our books or click the titles below!

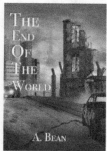

The Beta Rises
A. Bean

The Bite Of The Alpha
A. Bean

The Scribe
A. Bean

The Barren Fields
Valicity Elaine

Cross Academy
Cross Academy Book I
VALICITY ELAINE

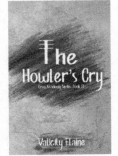

The Howler's Cry
Cross Academy Series Book II
Valicity Elaine

THE NINE BIRTHS OF CARNAGE
Cross Academy Book III
VALICITY ELAINE

THE TESTAMENT RELICS
Cross Academy Book IV
Valicity Elaine

I AM MAN
Valicity Elaine

I AM LOST
Valicity Elaine

I AM BROKEN
Valicity Elaine

I AM FREE
Valicity Elaine

I △M
COMPL=T=

Valicity Elaine

Withered Rose

Valicity Elaine

Clipping Thorns

Valicity Elaine

Fractured Diamond

Valicity Elaine

PATCHES

Valicity
Elaine

The I Word

Valicity Elaine

Made in United States
Orlando, FL
05 December 2023